MY DOG WAS A REDNECK, BUT WE GOT HIM FIXED

Roger Pond

Other Books by Roger Pond

It's Hard To Look Cool When Your Car's Full Of Sheep
Tales From The Back Forty
(Humor)

Things that go "Baa!" in the Night
Tales from a Country Kid
(Humor)

Take the Kids Fishing, They're Better Than Worms
Tales from a Country Kid
(Humor)

The Livestock Showman's Handbook:
A Guide to Raising Animals for Junior Livestock Shows
(Informational)

My Dog Was A Redneck BUT We Got Him Fixed

Tales from The Back Forty

ROGER POND

Pine Forest Publishing

First Printing, March 1997
Second Printing, May 1998
Third Printing, September 2000
Fourth Printing, September 2004

Library of Congress Catalog Card #96-72170

Publishers Cataloging-in-Publication Data

Pond, Roger, 1944-
My Dog Was A Redneck, But We Got Him Fixed
1. Humor
I. Title

ISBN # 0-9617766-4-1

Published by Pine Forest Publishing
314 Pine Forest Road
Goldendale, Washington 98620

Cover by Karen Whitman

Printed in the United States of America

To my dog, Pokey, who needs to be fixed if anyone does.

To Shawn,
Merry Christmas
2011

Love
Mom & Dick

TABLE OF CONTENTS

ACKNOWLEDGMENTS

These stories have appeared in newspapers throughout the United States and Canada that use *The Back Forty* column. “The Fruit Roll” and “The Old Hotel” appeared also in *It’s Hard To Look Cool When Your Car’s Full Of Sheep*, Copyright 1989, by Roger Pond. “What Now Brown Cow?” and “Mother Did It With Gravy” appeared in *Things that go “Baa!” in the Night,* Copyright 1992, by Roger Pond.

I am grateful to Karen Whitman for her artistic talent, creativity, and patience while designing the cover; as well as her unique gift for locating a redneck dog when we needed one.

Thanks also to Carol York and Pete Fotheringham of Gorge Publishing for expert design assistance and electronic page layout.

A special thanks to my wife, Connie, for tolerating all of those stories that may have been stretched slightly

••••• PLEASE NOTE •••••

This book contains fictitious names. Any resemblance of these names to those of people you may know is purely coincidental. These stories are not to be taken seriously.

How To Bury A Hamster

Nearly everyone likes animals. Amid all the talk about animal rights and animal welfare, it's well to remember that people who own animals are concerned with their health and well-being, regardless of whether these critters are pets or farm animals.

A friend was telling me about the bond between the old-time sheepherders and their dogs. In the days when the mountains were alive with sheep, a sheepherder and his dogs were on their own for weeks at a time. A good dog saved the herder great amounts of exercise and frustration in containing or moving a large band of sheep.

As a result, the herder became quite protective of his canine assistant, and each thought his was probably the smartest dog that ever spit-up in a camp wagon. When several bands of sheep and their herders were accumulated for lambing or shearing, there was the ever-present danger of a herder saying the wrong thing about someone else's dog.

An error such as this could escalate into a wild melee of snarling, growling, and biting — so violent the dogs often had to jump in and break it up. My friend says the goal was to get the sheep sheared, and everyone back on the range as quickly as possible, before such squabbles could arise.

I thought about this when my daughter brought her hamster to our house for burial. Laura had the hamster for several years, and old Bob was like one of the family. Giving him a proper burial seemed important.

It's only natural that she would bring the little guy to our place. We live in the country and have accumulated a small cemetery of creatures that have gone to that big exercise-wheel in the sky. Laura lives in town, and a pile of fresh dirt in her yard might be grounds for an investigation in this day and age.

But a hamster? What kind of grave should we dig for a hamster? I thought of the efficient, two-inch diameter hole produced by a soil sampler. A person could bury hamsters in a hurry with an outfit like that, but it just didn't seem quite right.

Likewise, a post-hole digger was deemed too mechanical and impersonal. We finally selected a shovel and constructed a grave about the size of a small pony; and the little hamster was laid to rest in a cardboard casket made by Nike — his grave marked with a 200-pound boulder.

Moments like these always remind me of the attachment people feel for their animals, and the futility of projecting one's beliefs and sentiments onto someone else.

This is best illustrated by a little girl whose kitten was run over by the delivery truck. The girl was crying something awful, and her grandfather was doing his best to console her.

Finally Grandpa said, "Don't cry, honey. Your kitty has just gone up to heaven to be with God."

The little girl looked up through her sobs and said, "Now, what do you suppose God wants with a dead cat?"

Tractor Parades

I wish they wouldn't do that. Several times each year I see photos of antique tractor parades and say to myself, "Hey, those tractors are newer than the ones I used to drive. Maybe I'd better lie down here, before I fall over and hurt myself."

You would think farmers would have more concern for their neighbors than to organize antique machinery shows with stuff that's newer than equipment some of us are still using. If they want to show off, why can't they drive something new!?

It's embarrassing to see people fixing up machinery and parading it around like that. Old tractors are like other antiques: They're always a big deal to folks who don't have to use them.

This week I saw a photo of the Central Iowa Two-Cylinder Club putting on a plowing demonstration. Some of the drivers were about my age, although they looked much older. (The midwestern sun is hard on people.)

These guys were out there, turning that black Iowa soil with some old John Deere A's and B's, and a couple of 70's. They were pulling three and four-bottom plows and grinning like they just invented agriculture.

Those old tractors were firing on both cylinders — "Ker-Pow, Ker-Pow, Ker-Pow-Pow-Pow!" — waking up neighbors for miles around.

Some folks think John Deere invented the two-cylinder "Johnny Poppers" just to embarrass the neighbors. They knew farmers would buy anything that announces who gets into the field first each morning.

Some farmers cheated by going out to start up their tractor; and then going back to bed.

I thought about calling the Iowa two-cylinder club to check on their membership requirements. It might be fun to talk with folks with similar interests.

That kind of organization can get pretty stuck-up, though. They'd probably want to know how old my John Deere is, and I'd have to admit I don't have one.

"You have to own a tractor to join the club," they'd say.

"I have an Allis Chalmers," I'd tell them. "Oh, it has to be a two cylinder tractor?"

"But my Allis only *runs* on two cylinders!"

That's the trouble with tractor clubs: They get so narrow-minded. It takes all the fun out of driving those old machines.

Anybody can drive a tractor that runs like it's supposed to. It takes skill to drive one that only runs when it feels like it.

You won't see my old Allis Chalmers in any tractor parades. She still plows the garden; but only if it's a nice day, and her plugs are dry, and she feels like it.

Plowing is about the only job Allis does these days. I guess it's one of those things that doesn't take much effort.

If it took any effort, she wouldn't do it.

The Memory Can

The hardest thing about writing a news column is answering the question, "Where do you get your ideas?" My favorite reply is, "The cat drags them to my door each morning." I wish I had something better.

Tough as this question is, it's not as hard as one I got several years ago, when a well-meaning lady asked, "Do you write that stuff yourself?"

Did she think I was too dumb to write it, or too smart to write it? Who knows?

The big-time writers never have to struggle with issues like this. They always have a profound thought or high-sounding phrase to justify their ideas.

A recent column from syndicated columnist Russell Baker credits his "memory vault" as the source of a penetrating thought. "It's also about family values, which is why it popped up out of the memory vault last week," Baker says.

Doesn't that sound powerful? A memory vault.

That's why I'll never be a big-time columnist. I can't afford a memory vault, and would probably forget the combination if I could. Or lock myself inside, to be found years later babbling about my childhood.

What I have instead is a memory can. It's as good as a vault, and it fits my personality better.

Of course a memory can doesn't sound impressive, like a vault. A person wouldn't write, "It's about family values, which is why it crawled out of my memory can this morning." The ring just isn't right.

A memory can has its advantages, though. I just bury it in the yard and dig it up when I need an idea. The vault people wouldn't understand, but there's something about a can in the yard that brings back memories.

The can is more secretive, too. "What can? I don't know anything about a can." It's pretty hard to ignore a vault.

The second advantage of a can is the contents tend to interact, producing brand new substances and ideas. Memories come alive in a can, but remain dry and stale in a vault.

Any youngster can tell us a person who puts several items in a can and buries it, is likely to find something different when he digs it up. When you excavate the can, certain objects will be missing, and others will be stuck together — oozing new substances.

Readers might wish to try this at home. Find an empty peanut can and insert several coins and a dollar bill.

Then go down to the road and get a flattened frog. Put the frog in the can with the money, and bury this in the yard for two or three months.

When you dig up the can, you will find the coins have turned green, the dollar bill will be gone, but you can spend the frog.

Try that with your memory vault, Mr. Baker.

Don't Feed The Fairy Diddles

"Oh, look at that pretty bird!" my wife said. "I wonder what it is? Where's my bird book?"

"That's a western tananger," I replied knowingly.

"I think you mean tanager," she said. "There's only one 'N' in tanager."

"It's a tananger to me," I said. "I'm from West Virginia, and I call 'em as I see 'em."

Actually, I'm not from West Virginia, but my education comes from that state. That's because most of my teachers were from West Virginia, and they had a special way of saying things.

My most vivid memories of the Appalachian dialect didn't come from my teachers, however. These recollections originate from the summer I worked with Dexter at the state park.

Dexter and I had one of those summer jobs created by the government. The main problem was whoever created the job forgot to create some work to go along with it; so Dexter and I had the nerve-racking task of doing half a man's work all by ourselves. We had a lot of time to talk.

Dexter taught me a bird can be anything you want it to. It might be a "tananger," a "bush robin," or a "scarley bird." If your word describes the bird, that's what it is. The possibilities are endless.

Dexter would see a bird flitting from tree to tree and say, "There sure are a lot of 'yaller-hammers' around this year. I'll bet it's going to be an early fall."

"A bunch of yaller what?" I asked.

"Yaller-hammers. Them woodpeckers. Don't you know what a yaller-hammer is?" he instructed.

I later learned 'yellow-hammer' is a common name for a flicker in some parts of the country; so Dexter wasn't just making this up.

Still, I was surprised when he shouted, "Look at them fairy diddles jumpin' through the trees!" I looked skyward, expecting to see Peter Pan swinging on a grape vine; but Dexter explained that red squirrels are called 'fairy diddles' in West Virginia. (The same squirrel we called 'bummers' in Ohio.)

The value of such descriptive language was reaffirmed many years later when I was talking with a weed scientist at the University of Idaho. The weed man said he stopped one day to ask a road crew about a particular weed he was surveying.

One of the crewmen said, "Nah, I don't think we've got any of them plants here, but there's a patch of weeds up the road I ain't never seen before. That plant looks just like a big, ol' scaley carp."

"A what?" the weed scientist asked.

"A big, ol' carp," the roadman said. "It looks like a big, ol' scaley carp."

The weed scientist drove up the road a mile or so, and sure enough, there was a patch of field pennycress — looking for all the world like a big, ol' scaley carp!

The weed man got a kick out of this, but it pretty much ruined his career as a scientist. To this day he can't even look at a field pennycress plant without calling it a "carp weed."

Tent Camping

I finally did it. I broke down and bought a new tent. I've learned over the years that a person either breaks down and buys a tent, or he buys the tent and breaks down later.

Either way, I've never seen a tent camper who wasn't broken down in one way or another.

I've always been fascinated by tents. Ever since I became old enough to hide in the woods, I've had two or three of these charming, little structures.

My first tent was an obstinate, little piece of canvas, referred to as a pup tent in those days. Mine was called a Mountain Pup Tent in the catalog.

The term "mountain pup tent" had a nice ring for my twelve-year-old mind; but I soon learned this structure was named for a small breed of dog found in the mountains. My first outing confirmed mountain pups are tiny, water-loving creatures, well-suited to sleeping under a wet piece of canvas.

My first tent taught me everything a person needs to know about camping:

1. You can't believe anything they tell you in the catalog.

2. There is no such thing as a waterproof tent.

The tent I bought this week is one of those modern, pop-up jobs. It's advertised as a "6 or 7 person family tent, with four zippered windows (including the door) for excellent ventilation."

The walls are "durable nylon taffeta," and the tent has two roof vents for added air movement. I think you get the picture: This tent is 80 percent ventilation.

I told my son, "This thing is so well-ventilated, you won't even know you're inside. If I wanted ventilation, I wouldn't need a tent!"

In addition to more air movement than a wind-tunnel, my new tent has "no-see-um mesh" in all the roof vents and windows. That's another thing I've never had in a tent.

Anybody who has been camping more than once knows there are things in the woods that would just love to get into your tent. From Ghoulies and Ghosties and long-legitty Beasties, Good Lord deliver us.

Tent campers have enough problems already without worrying about things they can't even see! Folks who worry about "no-see-ums" had better stay in the house, as far as I'm concerned.

There's no such thing as a "6 or 7 person family tent," either. Just try putting two adults and four kids in a tent and see what kind of family you've got when it's over. (Anybody with that many kids didn't get them by sleeping in a tent, anyway.)

To make a long story short, I bought the tent. Then I tried to set the thing up. That's the main test for any tent: Can you set it up?

The directions for this one say, "With a person at each front corner of the tent, flex the fiberglass pole into an upward position."

Are they crazy?! A person at each front corner? Where am I going to find someone crazy enough to go camping with me in a tent?!

That's insane. I'll just have to tie the tent to a tree and pull it up like I have all the others.

Transplanting Corn

I couldn't believe it; they were selling corn in flower pots! Who ever heard of buying sweet corn plants to put in your garden?

These weren't exactly flower pots, but those little plant containers one finds in a nursery. Some held five corn plants and others contained a single plant. The five-plant containers cost $1.79.

I couldn't find a price for the single plants, and I surely wasn't going to ask. Someone might think I was going to buy one!

This was my annual trip to the nursery with my wife. Connie goes to buy roses and bedding plants, and I tag along, reading the labels and grousing about prices. She tries to lose me as quickly as possible.

My wife visits the nursery often, but she only takes me about once a year. That's understandable, I guess.

The sweet corn was the object of my ire on this trip. I couldn't believe folks would pay good money for corn transplants. The crop is so easy to grow from seed or by starting plants in the house.

My mind raced back to the only time I can remember transplanting corn. It was 1956, and I was 12 years old. The old John Deere was fitted with duck-footed shovels in the front and smaller spring-tooth points behind the rear wheels.

I had just made the turn on the end rows and skipped over four rows to head back across the field. We had a two-row planter and a two-row cultivator in those days; so a person cultivating corn could make the turn as big as necessary — as long as he skipped an even number of rows.

A four-row turn was okay, and a six-row swing was fine, too; but skipping three rows or five meant you were on two separate planter laps, and the spacing wasn't always consistent.

A sixth grader should be able to count, of course, but he has other things to think about. He recalls the last shot of the basketball game, the proper weight line for casting trout flies, or the camping trip when the biggest bear you can imagine walked out of the woods with six little pigs.

All of these things were bounding through my mind when I looked over and noticed three rows between me and the previous pass with the cultivators. A glance between the wheels showed duck-feet digging up corn, and a quick peek to the rear showed this had been going on for some time. That's how I learned to transplant corn.

First you dig a hole, and then cover the plant's roots with dirt. Stalks that are cut in half, or don't have any roots remaining, are planted leaf-side-up and buried deeply. When these turn brown a few days later, Dad and the neighbors might think the corn borers got 'em.

It's a thankless job, transplanting corn — certainly not something I would recommend. Any 12-year-old kid can tell us about that.

Always Cover Your Ribs

This year's World Series reminded me how much baseball has changed over the years. The players are over-paid, tickets are over-priced, and it takes three announcers to describe a ground ball to the shortstop.

I remember when Peewee Reese and Dizzy Dean did the whole show by themselves. Ol' Diz even sang "Wabash Cannonball" during rain delays!

These modern players aren't what they used to be, either. I look at that big left-hander from Seattle and ask, "Hey, Randy, why don't you go get a haircut?"

I would ask this from a distance, of course. I learned about baseball, life, and fastball pitchers many years ago.

My instructor was a left-handed kid from Piqua, Ohio, and we all expected to see him in the big leagues some day. He was fast, and his pitches definitely had a tail on them.

His fastball was there for an instant, and then it was gone. All the batter saw was a little, white blur — with an awful, hissing sound behind.

I never could stay in the box against this kid. My mind

would say, "Stay in there. Stay in there." But my feet said, "The rest of you can stay if you want. I'll see you in the dugout!"

The only guy who tarried in the batter's box was our shortstop, Steve. Steve was a round-faced kid with big, thick glasses, giving him the appearance of Mr. Peepers in a baseball uniform.

In his yellow batting helmet, Steve looked like a construction worker with a Mason jar over each eye.

He was batting in the top of the eighth, and the first pitch was about a foot outside. Steve hit the dirt, anyway. The rest of us had been doing that all day; so there was no reason he shouldn't.

The second pitch was a curve, and he only jumped back a foot or two. The third was a strike, and Steve said to the umpire, "That one sounded a little high to me."

The rest of the team started yelling from the bench. "Stay in there, Steve! Be a man! You can hit him. Be ready for the next one!"

The next pitch started a foot-and-a-half inside and never changed course. Steve stood his ground, expecting this one would tail away like the rest of them.

It didn't, and he caught it right in the ribcage. Steve bent over and began staggering around the plate.

Tears fogged his glasses, as the umpire said, "Take your base, son," and Steve stumbled down toward third.

"Sorry. We can't give you that one," the ump said. "You'll have to take first."

Our coach finally got him down to first, and all of us "cheerleaders" on the bench were feeling kind of guilty. If we had kept our big mouths shut, this might not have happened.

That's when I realized baseball teaches one of life's big lessons:

When the game seems so sporting,
Your team is exhorting
And everyone's claiming first dibs,
You can kick in the dirt and snarl at the mound,
But always *cover your ribs!*

Wanted: Good Honest Biologists

The biologists must be on cloud nine these days. Within the past 30 years biology has been elevated from the perusal of frog innards to the foundation of society.

Nobody cared about biology when I was a kid. If someone said he wanted to be a biologist we figured he'd been playing with too many frogs.

But now we have spotted owls, short-nosed suckers, and green-eyed toads to worry about; and biologists are calling all of the shots. Biology has become so popular I'm thinking of coming out of the biological closet myself.

Readers may have trouble believing that I'm a trained biologist, but I have an M.S. in wildlife management. The fact I have little experience in that field is a point of concern, but many biologists don't have much experience. I know, I went to school with some of them.

We could take Fred, for example. Fred was researching habitat needs of the raccoon when I was in graduate school. We used to sit in the graduate room and trade hunting and fishing stories for hours.

Fred's research proved the raccoon needs a place to sleep and something to eat. Beyond that, they just don't give a rip about anything.

Fred told me an earlier study showed a severe decline in the raccoon population in my home state of Ohio during the 1930's and 1940's. Authors of this study reasoned that destruction of woodland habitat was the obvious cause.

Some years later, when the woodlots were nearly gone, the raccoon population recovered. Biologists found the critter had learned to sleep in hay lofts.

While Fred studied the raccoon, I stalked the Hungarian partridge for my graduate research. This bird was introduced to Ohio in the early part of the century and became quite plentiful during the 1930's and 1940's.

The Hungarian partridge has likely vanished from Ohio by now, and I swear it wasn't my fault. I couldn't find a single bird in the summer or fall of 1970; but a farmer found a nest of eggs, proving they still existed.

I concluded there was a lack of grit in prairie soils, making gravel roads an important part of partridge habitat. These roads had all been paved during the 1950's. (Don't laugh, I had to come up with something.)

An earlier study concluded the partridge needed hedgerows for survival. This researcher was from Denmark, where they had lots of hedgerows — as well as partridges.

Readers will recall the whitetail deer was nearly extinct in the corn belt states during the 1940s and '50s. This was generally attributed to habitat destruction by modern agriculture.

Today, whitetail deer are so plentiful in those states that farmers have to chase them from the fields so they can harvest a crop. The habitat certainly hasn't been restored as far as I can see; and many states have resorted to all-you-can-eat hunting limits in an attempt to thin the herds.

What causes these discrepancies in biological prediction? I certainly don't know. And I'm just waiting for some good, honest biologists to stand up and admit they don't know, either.

How To Train A Cat

I guess I'll never be a "cat person." There's something about cats that gets under my skin, and these animals know it.

I was standing in a book store a few months ago when the owner's kitty decided my leg would make a good rubbing post. The cat rubbed against my leg in one direction. Then he turns around and rubs the other way.

Yellow hair was piling-up on my pant-leg and I was thinking, "If this cat would just rub around toward the front of my leg, I'll bet I could loft him right through the gardening section."

The kitty knew he was safe, though. He had been lounging around that store his entire life and was pretty sure he owned the place.

The thing that bothers me most about cats is their attitude. These animals go to great lengths to convince their owners they can't be taught anything.

That's one of the misconceptions about felines. They aren't dumb. They can be taught, but it takes determination.

I've found the best aid to training cats is a tennis racquet.

Anytime my cat gets to acting a'fool I just show him my tennis racquet, and he straightens right up.

Another misconception about cats is that they are such clean animals. I don't know why sitting around licking yourself is considered clean, but that's the way some folks see it.

A third misunderstanding is that cats have nine lives. That rumor was started years ago by people who couldn't tell a dead cat from a live one.

I fell into that trap myself some years back — when we owned a big, white tom cat who didn't stay home very well.

One spring I noticed a white spot in the neighbor's alfalfa field and figured Old Tom had gone to his big banjo in the sky. The cat had been missing for several days, so I didn't mention the spot in the field for fear of upsetting the kids.

The white spot laid in that field for weeks — until the hay was baled and summer faded into fall. The spot disappeared about September — just before Tom came walking into the barn, looking like he had survived a hard night, several months of sleep, and two cuttings of hay.

Last, but not least, there is a fourth misconception about cats that dissuades me from being a "cat person." I'm speaking of the common belief that cats lick their feet so much they should be kept in the house to protect them from pesticides and fertilizers.

Cat advocates say these creatures might walk through an area where chemicals have been recently applied, and then ingest those substances by licking their feet. That makes sense on the surface, but folks who have studied cats as I have will see the fallacy involved.

I've watched our cats for years and noticed they really don't lick their feet that much. I can't speak for other people's pets, but I think our cat could walk through toxic chemicals until the cows come home and it wouldn't bother him a bit.

If he sat in those materials, on the other hand, they would kill him for sure.

Too Much Equipment

Fall is always a time of excitement for me. I remember as a boy going to bed the night before opening day of squirrel season — and lying awake for hours listening to the wind in the trees near my window.

Wind is bad for squirrel hunting, because it covers the sound of squirrels champing on nuts or rustling through the branches. Those were the days when a youngster could slip off to the woods at daybreak, bag a couple of squirrels and still catch the bus for school.

School was detrimental to squirrel hunting, too; but I always found a way to suspend my education for opening day.

My sixth grade teacher once asked why I was always absent the first day of squirrel season. I told him I thought it was a national holiday.

Fortunately this teacher was from West Virginia — where the entire squirrel season is considered a holiday. That was another place and time, though, and I haven't shot a squirrel in 20 years.

I've moved on to larger game. If it isn't big enough to cut into quarters and drag from the woods on a hay rope, I'm just not interested, anymore.

Most hunters progress through a series of stages as they mature. We learn to value the outdoor experience more than the quest for meat.

It's a good thing too, because some of us haven't killed anything in a long time.

The mature hunter often takes to the field with nothing but his camera. Not out of love for photography, but because he forgot everything else.

The veteran outdoorsman is less concerned with bagging his limit, than with finding someone to eat it. His heart beats less from excitement and more from exhaustion.

While younger hunters are practicing their steely gaze and the aura of ice-water in their veins, the veteran is more concerned with ice-water down his back. He strives to pack light, but makes sure his car has plenty of gasoline.

The experienced hunter knows there's no such thing as a waterproof tent, and that air mattresses make good life preservers. He understands why firewood is always wet, and how dead trees can grow several feet overnight if this will help them fall on your tent.

A mature hunter recalls the iron-clad rules of the outdoors: "Don't brag on your dog before the hunt," and "Never trust a skinny cook." He knows the value of good equipment and buys two of everything.

A man's last hunting trips are a sad thing. By the time a guy can afford all the stuff he really needs, he's probably too old to carry it around.

The Barn Jacket

The fashion designers are at it again. They've taken a simple little cotton coat, sewn a few buttons on it, and named it "the barn jacket."

Then, they put this flimsy, little coat on a pouty-faced model to show how adorable our children will look when we send them off to school in a brand new "barn jacket." Upscale department stores are offering these at $59 apiece.

Can you imagine that? They're selling brand new "barn jackets" to folks who don't realize what an ugly and disgusting garment a barn jacket really is.

Even fashion designers should know a barn jacket isn't a garment; it's a condition. It's like a barn hat, a barn shirt, a barn cat: It's a mess!

"Barn jacket" isn't a style. The word "barn" explains what happened to it!

The genuine barn jacket is covered with axle grease, dog hair, calf slobber, and other compounds fashion designers don't know much about. It's like a cowboy's hat. The one his dog sleeps with in the back of the pickup.

I had several barn jackets when I was a kid, and I can't imagine sending anyone to school in them. A coat like this has a special character only its owner can appreciate.

I've never seen a barn jacket with buttons, either. The calves chew those off in a matter of days.

My barn coats all had a zipper that was permanently stuck about half way between my navel and Adam's apple. I put them on arms first, and often wore them backwards as a matter of convenience.

I always took those jackets off before going into town. My brothers told me I might get into a car accident, and the ambulance people would see the zipper in the back — and try to turn my head around straight.

My favorite barn jacket was procured from the army by my older brother, Kenny. Kenny served in the infantry before the volunteer army took over; and like others of his era, he conscripted a couple of field jackets and some "Mickey Mouse" boots when he left the service.

That army field jacket was the best barn coat I ever had. It had a zipper, and buttons, and a removable liner for winter use.

Best of all, it had enough pockets for candy bars, musk-rat traps, shotgun shells, dead rabbits, a few fish, gopher bait, and a can of Bag Balm.

I finally had to throw the old army jacket away this fall. I hadn't worn it in quite awhile, and the buttons and zipper rotted off years ago.

I asked my wife to fix it, but she started looking for the matches instead of her sewing machine. The old coat still had its character, though.

That's the main reason we had to burn it. My barn jacket's character was getting so strong, I had to take a shower every time I took it off.

Roadkill In The Basement

I got a chuckle from a recent news article about security in rural courthouses. I don't know what causes it, but something in my personality makes me laugh about serious matters.

The news report says small town courthouses have begun putting up signs to tell visitors to leave weapons outside courtrooms. Some counties have banned all weapons from the courthouse and security buzzers have been installed in many government offices.

I know employee safety is a growing concern for public and private employers, but old memories of courthouse happenings continue to challenge my solemn demeanor.

I was lucky. All my years of government servitude were spent in county extension offices; and these are located at the far end of the courthouse, down in the basement, or in some godforsaken annex several blocks away.

Extension agents have it made when it comes to security. If anyone gets really mad at the county agent, he's pretty well cooled-off by the time he can find the office.

We didn't see a lot of riff-raff or people off the street, either. In most cases, they simply couldn't find us.

My desk was quite a distance from the sheriff's office, but that was never a great concern. I figured if someone thought I killed her house plants the sheriff probably wasn't going to protect me anyway.

Nobody had security buzzers when I worked in the courthouse, and I can see the wisdom in that line of thinking. The news article mentioned earlier says a maintenance official has fixed two bullet holes in one county courthouse during the past six years.

Both of these plaster wounds were caused by accidental discharges of firearms by sheriff's deputies. I don't know about you, but I would think twice before pushing an emergency buzzer hooked-up to one of those guys.

The main thing I remember about courthouse security was the way we treated trustees from the jail. The custodian was the jailer as well, and he was pretty good at finding chores for the inmates.

One of the choice jobs for the jail trustees was skinning out deer that had been killed on the road. Center-line venison was a staple on the jail menu in those days, and someone had to skin it out and cut it up.

Many times I have trudged down to the courthouse basement looking for a custodian, and there would be a deer carcass hanging from the ceiling and a couple of inmates whacking away with their butcher knives.

One day I was upstairs at the front desk in the sheriff's office, when a couple of jail trustees came trundling through — wearing those orange prisoner jumpsuits and pushing a cart filled with butcher knives and saws.

"We can't get the cart down the stairs, so Bill said to use the elevator," they told the deputy at the front desk. Then the trustees proceeded out the door and down the main hallway of the courthouse.

The deputy watched as the men in orange pushed their load of knives and saws down the public hallway and waited for the elevator to the basement. Then she turned around and said to me, "You know there's something about that picture that just doesn't look quite right."

Fancy Equipment

I guess I'll never get used to fancy equipment. I wouldn't mind trying. It would be nice to have some swell stuff where I could look at it on a regular basis, but I'm afraid I just couldn't adjust.

The main thing I have against fancy equipment is the price. I look at my old stuff and the cost of new equipment and conclude, "I know this old boat has some problems, but you'll have to admit it has a lot of character."

That's one of the reasons I didn't go to the sportsman's show this year. Those events are so disheartening. What's the use of walking around looking at a bunch of stuff you can't afford anyway?

Outdoor shows always remind me how far out of touch I've become with the world of sport. Times have changed since the days my brothers and I sauntered into our local hardware store in search of fishing rods.

I was only about six, and hardly big enough to saunter — but I did the best I could. My brothers were around 12 or 13, and they knew exactly what they wanted: They wanted the best fishing rods in the store, as long as they cost less than $5.

That was easy in those days. Our store only had four rods, and all of them cost less than $5.

The store owner saw us coming. We were barely inside when he pulled a glass rod off the rack and began whipping it around like a foil. Then he took hold of the tip and bent the rod double to show how flexible it was.

In retrospect, I think the store owner ruined every rod in the place just showing folks how flexible they were. This was all very impressive to three young boys, however.

My brothers left the store with two glass rods and the prettiest little "green hornet" reels you ever saw; and the whole set cost them $7.

We loaded those green hornets with 20 pound dacron, attached a half-pound of weight and a huge bait-hook, and created some of the ugliest bird's nests you ever saw. Those reels weren't very forgiving, but they sure were pretty.

The old bait-casting reels came to mind as I stood beside a fishing display at an outdoor show a couple of years ago. A friend and I were perusing some rods and reels when I absent-mindedly picked up a sleek, little fly reel.

The reel was obviously sound and well-made, but nothing fancy as far as I could tell. A gentleman in the booth asked if I had any questions about the reel, and I said, "Yeah, how much do they cost?"

"Well, the one you have there sells for two-ninety-five," he said. "We have a larger model for salt-water fishing that costs a little more."

"Two-ninety-five?" I wondered out loud. "This looks like a pretty nice little reel."

Noticing my surprise at the great price, my friend leaned over and said, "He means two hundred and ninety-five *dollars*."

I returned the reel carefully to the table — wiping my finger prints on my shirt, and stumbled off in search of more bargains.

If They Get Fat, Sell 'Em

No, I'm not on the Internet. At least I don't think I am. They can't make us be on it, can they?

All of this talk about Internets and "Information Super-Highways" makes me feel like a possum in the fast lane: Should I get excited and jump up and down, or just lay low and stay out of the wheel tracks?

Don't get me wrong. I own two computers and wouldn't be without either of them, but computers can't do everything.

I remember when the computer craze first hit. I was working for a university, and everyone was talking about computer technology.

The university bigwigs said, "Computers are the coming thing. We need to be on the cutting edge, expand the learning curve, and remain innovative within our projected evolution." The rest of us said, "What?"

But they bought us computers, anyway. These machines had ears on one side, where the user was obliged to plug his telephone receiver directly into the computer. It was like someone had designed a car and used a saddle for the front seat.

The bigwigs said, "Get with it. Send messages to each other and utilize this new technology."

"What technology?" I asked. "I've already got a phone."

Some folks sent messages anyway, but those missives weren't on the cutting edge as far as I could tell. That computer service was like a telephone you couldn't hang up, or having your junk mail opened and flung across your desk. You couldn't get away from it.

Later on, we got computer programs for farmers, and this was a breakthrough for me. The cattle ration program was my favorite.

This program permitted the user to enter the size and number of cows he was feeding, along with the activity those cows performed (breeding, gestating, lactating, etc.). Then, the user entered types of feeds available in his locality, and the computer devised the most economical ration for this group of cows.

Unfortunately, the only feeds available in my area were barley and alfalfa hay. So all I could ask is, "Should we give 'em more barley, or should we give them more hay?"

Generally, the cattle owner would say, "I can't afford barley, and I'm nearly out of hay. I'll just turn them out on pasture."

My old friend, Andy, had even fewer choices. Andy was a county agent on the coast. A man came into his office one afternoon and asked how hogs would do on a ration of fish entrails and cranberries.

It seems this fellow had a source for cull cranberries and a good lead on all the fish entrails he could cook and serve. Andy checked his computer and found nothing about fish innards or cranberries as a feed for anything. So he called the swine specialist at the university.

"Fish entrails and cranberries?" the specialist groaned. "Haven't those beachcombers you work with ever heard of corn and barley?"

"Well, what should I tell him?" Andy asked.

"I'll tell you what I'd tell him," the specialist said. "Tell him to feed those hogs all the fish innards and cranberries they'll eat; and if they get fat, sell 'em. If they get thin, give 'em some barley."

The Fruit Roll

Everyone knows teachers in this country are not paid what they are worth. Some are paid more than they're worth, and some are paid less.

We had the same problem when I was in school. In those days the community tried to mitigate the low salary received by teachers with favors designed to help them cope.

Many of our teachers were older ladies who were not married, so the neighbors or the school board or somebody would help them put up the storm windows, or give them a cord of firewood to help supplement their salary.

The old tradition of bringing the teacher an apple was founded on the same principle. Some say this also helped prevent scurvy in those areas where wild fruit was not normally plentiful.

But one of the most exciting rewards for teachers at my school was the "fruit roll." The fruit roll was kind of like a surprise party; but instead of bringing presents everyone brought some fruit.

Each kid would bring an orange or an apple or something

for the teacher; and when the signal was given everyone would roll their fruit up the aisle toward the front of the room. Then the teacher would have all of this fruit to take home.

I admit this tradition may have been short-lived. I have never talked with anyone who remembers a fruit roll, and I can recall only one such event during all of my years in school. (There's a good chance that was the last one ever held.)

It was Mrs. Hardy's fourth grade (not her real name), and all of the kids had packed some extra fruit in their lunches. Most of us had no idea what a fruit roll was all about, but we figured the organizers knew what they were doing.

Just before the signal was given to roll the fruit I could see we had a problem.

We'll call him Ed — and he was surely special. In those days we didn't have programs for kids who would benefit from special attention, but everyone knew Eddie needed extra consideration.

He had brought a banana for the fruit roll, and his seat was clear in the back of the room. You don't have to be a produce manager to know that bananas don't roll well.

The fruit roll was over as suddenly as it began. All at once there were apples, oranges, plums, you name it, rolling down the aisles and bouncing off the baseboards in the front of the room. There was a lot of bruise damage.

Eddie threw his banana half-way up the aisle, and another kid tossed it the rest of the way.

Mrs. Hardy became very emotional. I think she was trying to decide whether to thank the class or send the whole bunch to the office.

Wilderness Medicine

Anyone who enjoys the outdoors should be enthused about the new outdoor sports programs for women. I'm happy to see the value of such instruction is finally being recognized.

The Indiana Department of Natural Resources, for example, sponsors a program called "Becoming An Outdoor Woman," where women can attend a weekend of instruction on fishing, fly tying, dog training, and many other sports.

If a fellow could get his wife to attend a program like this, she might become interested in fishing and hunting — or learn how to tie up a few Carey Specials in the lantern light of the old fishing cabin. (I know it's a long shot, but there's nothing wrong with dreaming.)

Sponsors are quick to point out these outdoor programs are not just for wives; they're for any woman who wants to become more involved in outdoor sports. Women don't attend because husbands want them to, either.

That doesn't surprise me any. If a guy wants his wife to attend something like this, he'd better get it done in the first year of marriage as far as I can tell. After that, his best chance of getting her there is to tell her not to go.

I'm reminded of a woman describing her job to my wife a few months ago. "This is the worst job I've ever had," she said. "Everyone is always telling me what to do and then complaining about the way I do it. It's like going fishing with your husband."

My wife thought that was hilarious, but I didn't. Sometimes her sense of humor leaves me baffled.

Don't get me wrong, I think outdoor programs for women are a great idea — married, unmarried, or whatever. I wouldn't be surprised if single men are asking for the graduation list.

The class offerings are excellent, too. New sessions for the Indiana program include game calling, working dogs, rappelling, wilderness medicine, and kayaking.

I questioned the rappelling and kayaking at first, but I suppose these have some value. I can think of several instances where I've dropped a bird over a cliff, and someone who was good at rappelling would be a fine companion in those situations.

Kayaking skills would come in handy if a bear was swimming toward your boat and the little woman was obliged to use the oar on him. Or for those times when a person is camped in the swamp and someone has to swat mosquitoes with her canoe paddle.

I was especially happy to see the class on wilderness medicine. The value of this subject was impressed upon me and some elk-hunting friends many years ago.

My two friends and I arrived in camp with two tents and one stove; and somehow decided to put the stove in the cook tent and sleep in the cold, clammy one. Then, we pitched our sleeping tent with the door uphill — so the melting snow would trickle in and float our sleeping bags.

Next, I got out some steaks for dinner — with the plan of cooking them outside under the tent flap. The cold rain and snow turned my steak-grilling job into a two hour ordeal. Dinner was late that evening.

My friends and I laugh about that outing nearly every time we see each other. Even after all these years, everyone agrees, if we had packed a couple more pints of wilderness medicine, that might have been a pretty good trip.

School Shopping

I read an amusing article recently about choosing a school for your children. It wasn't supposed to be amusing, but it was for me.

The modern trend is to case-out the schools when moving to a new location. That way folks can buy a house in the right area, thereby deciding which school their kids will attend.

Nobody even thought of shopping for a school when I was a kid. That would be like choosing your parents. Kids just went to school where they were born.

If your parents moved, you went to a new school; but you never had a choice. If we had a choice, most kids would have chosen no school at all. So parents didn't talk much about options.

Nowadays parents spend weeks visiting schools and interviewing teachers and principals to decide where little Alphonse will learn his ABC's. It's too bad the school doesn't have a choice. They might like to send little Alphonse somewhere else.

Besides, there's no point in talking to teachers and principals when choosing a school. If it were me, I'd bypass the teachers and principal and go straight to the janitor. That's the person who knows what's going on.

Teachers may come and go, but custodians are there for the long-haul. If you want to learn something, the janitor is the guy to see.

Harry was our janitor when I was a kid, and everyone knew he ran the school. If someone wanted to use the gym, Harry opened the doors.

If something broke, he fixed it. When the principal forgot his key, Harry let him into the school.

Nothing is more poignant than an administrator begging the janitor to let him into the building. We kids stood in the background shouting, "Don't do it, Harry! Don't let him in."

I've forgotten some science teachers and two or three superintendents, but I'll always remember Harry. He would enter the furnace room just as an eraser went sailing past and ask, "What are you boys doing in here?"

"We're just cleaning these erasers," we would tell him. "Harold must be turning the crank too fast, and this machine keeps throwing them out."

Harry knew there was an eraser fight in the furnace room. The old janitor never got upset, though. Our school building had been around a long time, and Harry probably put a little chalk dust on those walls himself.

He would look at our pile of erasers and ask, "Where did you boys get all of these?"

We explained our technique of going room to room, collecting erasers. "All of the teachers seemed happy to get rid of them," we told him.

Harry never said so, but the twinkle in his eye was clear enough. He knew how Harold and I got that eraser cleaning job: All of the teachers were perfectly happy to get rid of us, too.

Pretty, Brown Ribbons In The Snow

It's easy to forget how much agriculture has changed over the years. Production levels have changed, techniques have changed, and most of all, the equipment has changed.

I was reminded of these things recently when I walked into a modern, swine farrowing barn to photograph baby pigs. There they were, 10 or 12 pigs to a litter, all lined-up and attacking their dinner.

Some say confinement farrowing systems are cruel to animals, but I see them as much more humane than older methods of production. Modern swine systems restrict the sow's movement, which helps keep the baby pigs warm, well-fed, and safe from the shuffling hooves and wafering impact of a 500-pound sow.

Good riddance to the days when we headed for the woods with a bucket of wet grain (slop) and a trough to feed the old sow who opted for a bed of leaves under a paw paw tree — rather than the nice A-frame house we had provided for her.

If being stepped-on or otherwise mashed by a sow makes a pig feel good, I suppose some of those woods pigs were happier than the modern ones. I know a lot of them never survived until they got to the barn.

I can also remember a few Saturdays when my brothers and I were coerced into entering the old hog barn with a pitchfork and a shovel to throw manure into the spreader parked outside.

At times like these a boy learns if he wants to heal people, he should become a doctor. If he wants to relieve suffering, he should be an agricultural engineer.

The hard part of cleaning the hog barn was throwing the stuff through a window that was a little too high and just slightly smaller than the shovel. If you tilted the shovel, the manure ran down the handle; and if you threw it too hard (or missed the window), you had better have your mouth closed. We didn't talk much when cleaning the barn.

Readers who have cleaned those old barns will remember the pitchfork was for the thick stuff and the shovel was for the thin. The old wedding vows "through thick and thin" had some real meaning in those days.

There was nothing glamorous about cleaning the old barns. My father taught me that becoming sentimental about hog manure is a big mistake, also.

I will always remember a farm writer's attempt to make something poetic out of barn-cleaning day. The writer's husband was busy cleaning the barn one late February day when she wrote, "I watch through the kitchen window, as Herman loads the manure spreader and makes pretty, brown ribbons in the snow."

My father read that and nearly fell out of his chair. "Well, isn't that something?" he said. "Most of us just haul the manure; but Herman uses it to make pretty, brown ribbons in the snow!"

Nouveau Riche And the Four Squares

It's that time of year again. Time to figure our taxes. I began calculating business income and taxes this week — and finally gave up in disgust. I'm giving it to our accountant in the hope she will hold the news until April.

Tax time always reminds me of an old friend who used to work in the post office. When folks mailed their tax forms April 15, Mike would tell them, "Don't forget. There are millions of people in the world who would love to pay taxes in this country."

A lot of people wanted to leap over the counter and get him for that, but he was probably right. It would be hard to find a better place to live, despite our hand-wringing about taxes.

I've always thought the taxes we pay are far less important than other measures of prosperity. I grew up in a time when toilet paper was the benchmark for financial success. The middle class didn't just go out and buy ten rolls of toilet paper at a time like we do now.

Readers of my generation will remember the first thing a person learned in potty training was how to tear off two squares of toilet paper at one time. Poor folks used only one, and rich people probably used three or four; but my family was middle class. We always tore two at a time.

Mother was strict about the two squares rule. I can remember going into town to play with friends, and the town kids would take a roll of toilet paper and just reel off a big wad. I would think, "Now, there's a kid who's never going to amount to anything."

The country had plenty of toilet paper in those days, but we knew we couldn't afford to waste it. This was before there were lots of wealthy people or yuppies and such. People who suddenly came into a lot of money were known as "Nouveau Riche" or simply the "Four Squares."

But then came the 1950's, when farm commodity prices went sky high. The national economy reached a point where a kid could go to work for "$1 an hour and three squares a day." The town kids thought "three squares" meant meals, but the farm boys knew better.

That's the main reason I went to college: The dream of a better life and a chance to use three squares of toilet paper. I'm not sure when the economy reached that level, but just a few years ago I realized I could tear off more than two at a time if I wanted to. Times like this cause a person to pause and take stock — and recognize how much our country has changed.

We took a trip to Canada a few years ago and witnessed the terrible fix that nation has gotten itself into. In addition to the high taxes and gasoline prices, the Canadians have made their toilet paper so narrow a normal person can't use it. A guy can use all of the squares he wants, but the roll's only two-inches wide!

Talk about an underhanded Tory trick. Anyone who thinks our government is in bad shape can just look north for the road to ruin.

Thoughts like this return each year when I work on my taxes. I consider it a time for reflection and review. My wife thinks it's a form of mental illness.

Real Men Don't Eat Lettuce

I am not the kind of person who tries a lot of new foods. If I have my eggs scrambled, rather than over easy, that's about as adventurous as I get when it comes to food.

When I go to a steak house, I get steak; or I'll have spaghetti and meatballs if we visit an Italian restaurant.

This drives my wife crazy. "That's okay," I tell her. "I like spaghetti and meatballs. When I don't like it, anymore, I'll quit ordering it."

A few weeks ago, we visited our favorite Italian restaurant. I studied the menu for a long time and then said, "I believe I'll try the spaghetti and meatballs. Do you remember if I usually get the regular sauce, or the spicy Italian?"

"It doesn't matter," Connie said. "Maybe if you get something different, you'll find you like it."

So I got the spicy Italian — and I didn't like it. I wasted an entire meal eating the wrong spaghetti sauce! You won't catch me doing that again.

That's the way I grew up. My mother was an excellent cook, but she had seven kids.

If Mother said we were having spaghetti and meatballs, that's what we were having. There wasn't any fooling around with "What else is on the menu?"

Folks didn't go to restaurants very often in those days, and people with seven kids didn't go to restaurants at all. We grew up on meat and potatoes — and whatever was doing well in the garden.

My family's eating habits provided a good laugh for one of my brother's neighbors some years ago. My brother's five-year-old was visiting the neighbors; and when the salad was passed at dinner, John didn't take any.

The lady of the house said, "Don't you want some salad, John. It's good for you."

"Men don't eat lettuce," the boy said. Obviously he had been watching his dad.

I can't speak for John, but I've tried some lettuce — and even recently branched out into Chinese food. There's an excellent Chinese restaurant in town, and we've learned they have a very economical "take-out" menu.

The food is great, but those who aren't used to Chinese take-out should be sure to remove it from those little bait buckets before serving. We used to get crickets and redworms in containers like those.

The old saying about being hungry an hour after a Chinese dinner is a bunch of baloney. You just have to know what to order.

Our local restaurant has a special that lets the customer choose four items. We started out ordering barbecued pork, pork fried rice, egg rolls, and chicken subgum. (The chicken subgum includes some veggies.)

Later on, we substituted sweet and sour pork for the chicken subgum. Sure, we lost the veggies, but so what? Rice is a vegetable where I come from.

Now, I tell my wife, "Okay, let's get the barbecued pork, pork fried rice, sweet and sour pork, and the egg rolls. And see if there's any way we can get some pork in those egg rolls."

Stole It From The Old Man

I guess I should have known. It's fine to give things to your kids, but a person should keep a record. Otherwise, you are constantly trying to remember what's yours and what's theirs.

That's what happened to me last week, when I said, "Hey Russ, I need to stop by your place and pick up my .22 rifle. The ground squirrels are becoming quite a problem around here."

"Do you mean that old bolt action?" he asked. "You gave that to me 10 years ago."

"Well, how about the 16-gauge?" I stammered. "Who does that belong to?"

"You gave me that, too, but you're welcome to borrow it back," he offered.

When Russell was a kid I always said, "There's no need to spend a lot of money on new hunting and fishing equipment. Why don't you just borrow mine? I'm not using it now, anyway."

So I loaned him a few things and gave him some more; until now the kid has more toys than I do. I have to go borrow them back!

I'm starting to recoup my losses, though. I borrowed some of Russ's golf clubs this summer. It's only a matter of time until I'll have the whole set.

It's called the "doctrine of adverse possession" in legal circles. This precept says a person who uses your property for a certain period of time (without you catching him) can claim legal interest — providing his lawyer is better than your lawyer, of course.

My son must have a good lawyer. He has gotten a lot of my stuff that way.

Principles such as these have ruled my family for generations. My dad loaned his kids cars, tools, hats, and houses. It's only natural we should do the same for our own.

There's a touch of heredity in the way we relate to our children — and our parents. My friend, Dick, would attest to that.

Dick was looking for his favorite cartridge belt some years ago, and he wasn't having much luck. He turned the house upside down looking for that belt. His nerves were on edge when his wife finally heard him kicking and grumbling through the den.

"What are you so upset about?" she asked.

"I can't find my leather cartridge belt!" he said. "The kids must have borrowed it. I'll probably never see it again."

"So, what's the big deal? Why don't you just buy another one?" she suggested.

"I can't buy another one," he groused. "They don't make them anymore."

"Well, where did you get that one?" his wife asked.

"I stole it from my old man!" he said.

They Taste Like Licorice

It's amazing what a person can do with a little grant money. Today I read about a project called the "Veterinarian Sun Protection Study," conducted by the National Farm Medicine Center in Marshfield, Wisconsin.

The project was funded by a grant from the Wisconsin Farmer's Cancer Control Program. That organization received the money from the National Institute of Occupational Safety and Health.

Anyone want to guess where the National Institute of Occupational Safety and Health got the money? It wasn't from any bake sale, you can bet on that.

It seems there's so much grant money around these days, folks are staying awake nights, trying to think up new ways to spend it.

The Veterinarian Sun Protection Study was supposed to determine if farmers and ranchers would object to receiving human health information from their veterinarian. The project involved 1,503 farmers and ranchers, each of whom received educational brochures about skin cancer.

Some got the brochures from their veterinarian, while others got them through the mail. The researchers then asked these cooperators if getting this material from a veterinarian was just as good as getting it through the mail.

Most said, "Sure." They didn't care how they got it. They said the vets are nice people and can deliver brochures just fine, as long as they keep them out of the manure.

Isn't it amazing folks can get a grant for something like this? Everybody knows rural residents have a very high regard for their veterinarian. Many of us have been weaseling medical advice out of our vet for years.

We call the vet out to look at an old horse, and then say, "What do you think, Doc? Do you suppose that bare spot on his head is the same thing I've got here on my arm?"

The vets are savvy about this kind of thing, though. They won't tell you anything, unless you can show them an animal that has the same symptoms.

The most notorious case of such medicinal monkey-business is credited to a ranch woman in Montana, who called the vet out to look at her bull. Breeding season had just begun, but the bull didn't seem all that interested.

So the vet gave ol' Bullwinkle a complete physical, but he couldn't find a thing wrong. The critter seemed a little dull, but physically, he was fine.

The vet told the rancher lady, "I don't see anything wrong with your bull. He probably just needs a little boost in his libido. I've got some pills in the truck that will take care of that."

The Doc said, "Give him two of these in his feed each day, and you'll likely see a big difference within a week."

A couple of weeks later, the woman's husband stopped by the vet's office and told the receptionist, "My wife asked me to stop by and get some more of those pills Doc left on his last visit."

"The vet won't be back 'til tomorrow," the receptionist said. "What kind of pills were they?"

"I don't know what he calls 'em," the man said. "But they're small, and green, and taste like licorice."

I'll Pass On The Chicken

There's nothing like a big power outage to remind us how nice it is to have electricity. Our most recent breakdown lasted less than a day, but some folks lost power for three days or longer.

My wife and I have a wood stove, and a fireplace, and a number of options for dealing with cooking and water shortages. Never-the-less, it's embarrassing to stumble around the house, flipping-on light switches — when you know darned well the juice has been off for hours.

Power outages are a serious problem for many businesses and some households, but just a minor inconvenience for others — as long as they don't last too long.

I remember a fellow who was running for office with a local utility back in the 1970's. One of his suggestions for conserving electricity was that people who own clothes dryers should pay a higher rate for their power.

He didn't get far, as I recall. Anyone who thinks Bob Dole had trouble with the women's vote should have seen the ballots for this guy.

The old-timers can tell us what it was like to run a farm or household in the days before electricity was available in rural areas. It was hard work, I'm sure of that.

An old friend once told me about the time he and his dad got snowed-in on their ranch. His mother had gone to town, and the snow got so deep she couldn't get back home.

His mom was the lucky one in that instance. It was six weeks before the snow melted enough for her to drive back to the ranch, and she wouldn't have been happy confined to the house all of that time.

My friend's mother had provided for her men, though. They had plenty of fruit and jelly — and a large supply of chicken, canned a few months before.

The two men ate canned chicken until it was coming out their ears. They boiled it, stewed it, fried it, baked it in the oven, and formed it into pies.

If anyone wants to write a book called, "A Million and One Uses for Canned Chicken," this man has the research.

This was before electricity was available in remote areas, but the two men hooked-up an old car light to a battery so they could read. (I don't know if that's possible, but that's the way I remember the story.)

Then, after a few days, the battery went dead and their reading passed away with it.

The ranch was down in the bottom of a canyon — where it gets dark about 4:30 each evening and daylight comes around 8:00 A.M. Anyone who isn't used to 14 hours of sleep gets a little stir-crazy after his 35th dinner of canned chicken.

I think of my old friend every time we have a power outage. The first thing I do is head outside and bring in several armloads of wood.

Then, I get the wood stove fired-up so we can heat some water for coffee. Finally, I look through the cupboards and say to myself, "Thank God, we're out of canned chicken."

The Old Hotel

Everyone agrees that change is healthy for a small community. We have to change in order to survive and prosper.

When times are tough it helps to look at other communities that have weathered economic hardship and somehow managed to flourish. The little town where I grew up is a good example.

I grew up near St. Paris, Ohio, and like most small towns ours always had a hard time attracting and holding industry. Maybe it was just bad luck, but many residents thought the problem went deeper than that.

Much of St. Paris was leveled by fire in 1883, resulting in the loss of 13 homes and almost the entire business section. Estimates of the damage were in excess of $105,000. (I told you it wasn't a big town.)

One example of the town's bad luck was the carriage factory that made St. Paris famous during the 1880s. Founded by a sign painter and his partner, the carriage factory reached its zenith in the 1890s.

The company exhibited their line of pony wagons at the World's Fair in Chicago in 1893, and soon began marketing these little surreys worldwide.

Then someone invented the automobile. Talk about bad

luck! Just when the town's economy gets hitched-up with ponies, Detroit cuts the traces.

St. Paris learned an important lesson from the pony wagon business: "A community's future is too important to get hooked up with the rear end of a horse."

Once the pony wagons were gone it was only a matter of time until the old hotel went with them. That was a shame, because the old Cline Hotel had such a rich history.

According to the History of St. Paris, by Kathleen Kite Brown, one Uncle Hiram Long moved into the Cline Hotel as a young man in the mid-1800s; he then proceeded to occupy the same room, and sleep in the same bed for over 50 years.

The history doesn't say why the proprietor never got Hiram a new bed, but I suppose he had his reasons.

The hotel was quite a landmark and was still standing when I was a boy. I remember signs on the door stating the building was condemned and would probably fall on anyone dumb enough to enter.

St. Paris was always a quiet, little town, but the town history states there was some excitement one night in the late 1800s. It seems a man from Zanesville decided to commit suicide at the Cline Hotel. This poor fellow slit his throat, and then jumped out the window of his hotel room.

That should be a lesson for anyone not familiar with small towns and old hotels. The Cline was only two stories tall.

This unfortunate man found his way back into the hotel lobby, dressed in his night clothes and covered with blood. Two doctors were called in, but couldn't save him.

In the final analysis no one could save the old hotel, either, and it's probably just as well. The town finally had the old building torn down in the 1960s.

After the hotel went down, some folks wanted to build a motel and attract some tourists, but small town politics put the kibosh on that. Each time the subject of a motel came up, someone would mention the old hotel and the man from Zanesville; and everyone would just lose interest.

Country Doctors

The debate over national health care shows how far we've progressed in the field of medicine. We've gone from the days when you hoped the Doc could cure what ails you, to the present when we expect good health regardless of what it costs.

Those who can remember the days when doctors made house calls must be surprised to learn a person can't get into the hospital without proof of insurance. This isn't the doctors' fault of course, doctors are as dedicated as ever; but our expectations for health care have surely changed over the years.

I'm not as old as I sound, but I can remember the days when doctors went to the house because folks were too busy, or too poor, to go to the doctor.

The country doctor did his best with what he had — and that usually wasn't a whole lot. Then, he got paid with what the patient had; and that wasn't much, either. Many a doctor went home with a few loaves of bread or a basket of green beans in payment for a long night's work.

When I was a kid, our doctor was a kind but intense

looking fellow with big, brown eyes that seemed to look right through a person. While his manner was comforting enough, Doc's unblinking stare always gave me the feeling he could x-ray your chest without any machinery.

I can remember going to the Doctor's office after school and waiting apprehensively for his door to open and his nurse to announce, "You can come in now, Roger. The Doctor has found a brand new package of those great, big needles."

Of course the nurse never said that. There would have been a hole in the waiting room wall if she had.

The old country doctor had a different philosophy from the physicians we visit today. Today's doctors emphasize preventive medicine and a healthful lifestyle, but the old-timers treated you for what ailed you and figured the rest would have to take care of itself.

The old doctors wouldn't lecture you about your smoking or suggest you should get more exercise. They'd just tell you what was wrong with you. A man could go into the doctor's office and say, "I've got this wheezing sound in my chest, Doc. What do you suppose is causing it?"

The Doc would say, "It's your lungs." He wouldn't ask how much you smoke or suggest you donate your leftover organs to science.

The modern doctor on the other hand, encourages exercise and healthful living. He might suggest you take up jogging or get out on the road to do some walking.

That might work for some people, but it won't work for retired farmers and folks who have lived in the country all their lives. If you walk down the road in the country, the neighbors will stop to offer you a ride.

Then, you'll spend the rest of the day trying to convince them you aren't running away from home.

My Dog Was A Redneck

I may be a bit of a redneck. I'm always more comfortable around loggers and cowboys than in the company of those other folks I call "city people."

Where I grew up, a redneck was just a person with an uneven suntan. We got that way because our hats protected our heads, and everybody's shirt collar was rolled up to exclude the dust and chaff. Only the neck got tan.

A person who went into the field without a hat and a long-sleeved shirt was considered some kind of dummy, in those days.

Some folks may be offended by the redneck image, but I'm not. That's the nature of the beast. If you can be offended, you're not a redneck.

I'll always remember a story a wheat farmer told me some years ago. This fellow often employed college kids during wheat harvest, and one year he hired a young man who was a cheerleader at a major university.

This kid was the opposite of a redneck. He showed up in the field wearing shorts and tennis shoes. Then, he did a few stretching exercises and proceeded to coat himself from ankles to ears with suntan lotion. The combine operator nearly fell out of the cab.

This young fellow was so upbeat and cheerful, you couldn't get mad at him; and even if you did, it probably wouldn't do any good.

My favorite redneck story involves a woman who used to visit our family when I was a kid. We'll call her Julia to protect the innocent, the blameless, and the near guilty.

Julia had a heart of gold and a happy way of making outrageous statements, completely by accident. All of us kids would gather round when she came to visit.

Like many of her generation, Julia didn't care what she said, as long as people understood what she meant. Deciphering what she really meant was her husband's job.

Howard (not his real name, either) was always nearby to correct misstatements and improve clarity. He was never stumped as far as I can remember.

Julia would be describing her sister's illness: "The doctor thinks Gladys is doing better," she said. "He gets the results of her autopsy next week."

Howard would think for a second and say, "Biopsy."

One day Julia's car wasn't running. "The mechanic says it will cost around $80. There's something wrong with the fuel rejecter," she said.

She spoke about people whose wages had been garnished, and a woman who had her nymph glands removed.

One visit Julia described a puppy Howard bought her in town. "That dog is such a redneck, we can't leave him in the house," she said.

"The dog is a roughneck," Howard interjected.

"Howard thinks we should have him tutored, but I don't see how that would help. What do you think?" she asked.

Her husband looked puzzled. Finally, he smiled faintly and said, "She means 'fixed'."

Don't Clone The Sheepherders

I'm starting to have second thoughts about this genetic engineering research. It's fine to tinker around with plants to develop disease resistance, or immunity to certain herbicides; but when scientists start fooling with the genetic make-up of animals, they are in over their heads.

This week I read scientists in Scotland have discovered how to make large numbers of identical sheep. These scientists claim this will be good for research where duplicate animals are in demand.

Others say the process could allow mass production of gene-altered animals, such as pigs with "humanized organs" suitable for transplanting, or sheep with better wool, superior meat, and more brains.

The Scottish researchers collected a nine-day-old sheep embryo, let the cells divide in culture dishes, and in less than a week they had thousands of identical sheep cells. Those cells were later implanted into unfertilized and de-geneticized eggs collected from ewes.

There's more to it than that, and I wouldn't try this at

home, but you get the idea. Let's just say these fellows went to an awful lot of trouble compared to just turning out the ram.

Isn't that just like a Scotsman? They're too darn cheap to buy a decent ram, so they try to clone the sheep they already have!

It all sounds harmless enough on the surface, but anyone who knows anything about sheep can see these scientists are barking at the wrong end.

If you're going to manufacture sheep, you certainly don't want them all alike. If they are identical, they'll all die on the same day!

Then what would you have? You'd be out of business in no time.

People who raise sheep are smarter than that. They try to get them as diverse as possible.

That's why we've got tall ones, short ones, black ones, white ones, smart sheep, and dumb sheep.

It helps the owner tell them apart, and the critters don't all get their heads stuck in the fence at the same instant. Let me tell you, there's nothing more disgusting than a bunch of sheep running around with a fence on their heads.

Those people in Scotland have had sheep around for thousands of years. You would think they'd know better.

The story I read says the Scots only produced five live lambs — after months of dividing up cells and fooling around. Three of the five lambs died the first few days after birth.

Welcome to the sheep business! Even a sheep scientist can learn something from that.

I don't know what it's going to take to stop some of these scientists. The news article says some have suggested human embryos could be cloned with the same methods used for the sheep.

Cloning humans is illegal in the United Kingdom, but who knows what these guys might try next.

I don't know about you, but the thought of five thousand identical sheepherders gives me the willies.

Some Disasters Just Aren't Natural

This has been a good year for disasters: hurricanes, drought, floods, you name it. Congress has been so busy with disaster relief they've hardly had time to collect the taxes.

Don't get me wrong. I'm in favor of disaster relief. My only objection is that relief is always limited to natural disasters: floods, hurricanes, hail, etc.

Just for once I'd like to see some relief for "unnatural disasters." Such as a sixteen-year-old with his first car, a bull in the milking parlor, four pigs in your wife's mini-van. Nobody helps with that kind of stuff.

Most of all I'd like to see disaster relief for vehicle towing. Of all the calamities I've ever been involved with, towing vehicles ranks near the top.

Everyone knows the drill. Something breaks down, gets stuck, or won't start, and we go find a vehicle to pull it with.

Then the second rig gets stuck, won't start, etc., and we find something else to pull that one with. By the time we're finished, a $50 problem has grown to a $500 disaster.

That's what happened recently when I tried to jump-start our Ford Bronco from the pickup truck. By the time I got the Bronco started, the truck had died. Then, when I tried to start the truck, its starter jammed, and that rig wouldn't run, either.

"No problem," I thought. "I've still got one vehicle left. (A

Subaru station wagon.) If I can pull the truck about 40 feet with the Subaru, I can coast it down the hill and start it that way."

I didn't have a driver for the second vehicle; but I was only going a short distance, the ground seemed level enough, and I had a 12-foot chain.

Everything went fine for a while. I drove about 10 feet and walked back to the truck to turn the wheels a little straighter. Then I got back into the Subaru and pulled the truck a little farther.

That's when I sensed an unnatural disaster in my future. There was a tiny, little knoll between the truck and the station wagon. When the truck passed over the knoll, it began picking up speed.

I looked back just in time to see the big, yellow beast gaining on me! And there was only 20 feet of driveway left.

I drove as far as I could and stopped the Subaru. The Subaru stopped the truck — with one of those crunching sounds so familiar to folks employed in wrecking yards.

This got my adrenaline up. Now I had the strength to push the truck by hand! I pushed it out to the brink of the hill in our driveway, jumped in, and coasted it a few feet. Then I learned I couldn't make the sharp turn in the drive and would have to back up.

But the truck's starter was stuck. So I couldn't back up. And if you think I'm dumb enough to tow it again, you know me better than I thought. I wouldn't try it alone, though.

The next morning, my wife and I used the Subaru again to tow the truck a few feet uphill. Then I could make the turn and coast down the drive.

We burned the clutch out of the Subaru in the process. It seems Connie didn't understand you can't release the clutch on a vehicle that isn't going anywhere — and let it continue slipping.

Readers will be happy to learn I explained this to her without yelling, getting mad, or anything. It was I, after all, who got the vehicles into that fix.

Besides, she hasn't noticed the dent in the Subaru, and I'd just as soon forget the whole thing.

Old Farmers Never Change They Just Take Longer Naps

Sometimes I wonder if education is a good thing. There's no question basic education (grade school, high school, college, etc.) is a societal benefit. But education just for the sake of more instruction and new degrees must certainly have a limit.

I can remember my dad coming into the house after talking with a man who had a great amount of education, and saying, "You know, that fellow is so smart, he's stupid."

That was Dad's way of saying, the guy has a brain-full of information, but no common sense to help apply it. Formal education and common sense aren't mutually exclusive, of course, but one doesn't guarantee the other.

My example for today is a Cornell University study of farmer efficiency. This research was based upon the common belief that a farmer's productivity increases with age until he or she reaches a peak in middle-age and then decreases until the poor, old codger isn't doing a blamed thing.

This has widespread implications, according to those who asked for the money. "Even the international competitiveness of the nation's farmers is a concern because the average age of U.S. farmers is increasing each year," they suggest.

The study assumes farmers within a region use about the same technology, but farmers of various ages might apply the technology differently. In addition, farmers might gain or lose efficiency as they purchase more land and become older, richer, and more senile. (They didn't say that exactly.)

The project learned that farmer efficiencies often decrease after a certain age, but this differs by region. Farmers in the West show more productivity increase up to 35 to 44 years of age, and less decline after that, than farmers in other regions.

Farmers in the Corn Belt exhibited no increased efficiency up to middle-age, but lost efficiency in later years. Farmers in the Northeast showed high increases early, and then lost their zip as they got older.

What does all this tell us? Nothing everybody didn't know in the first place.

Ranchers in the West are bound to take a long time to reach peak efficiency. They've got to find the horses, saddle them up, put the dogs in the pickup, and pull some grain drills out of the mud before they can do anything. It takes a few years to get all of that organized.

Corn Belt farmers, on the other hand, are so efficient when they start farming, the only way they can go is down. Besides, it gets hot and muggy in the Corn Belt. (I'm no farmer, but I know hot and muggy affects me a lot more than it used to.)

Farmers in the Northeast have always started out like a house a-fire, but then fizzled-out around lunch time. Anyone who gets up at 4:00 A.M. every morning to milk a string of cows, is bound to lose some bounce in their twilight years.

This just brings me back to my original thesis. Only a person with a huge amount of education would go to that much trouble to determine how farmers change as they get older.

Everybody knows, they don't change at all. They just take longer naps!

Working Out

Winter is tough. It's tough whether you live in frosty New England or sunny Florida. Winter gets us down because most of us don't get enough daylight or adequate exercise during the winter.

Scientists have proven that shorter days of winter affect the pituitary glands of animals, causing bears to hibernate, chickens to lay fewer eggs, and people to become grouchy. Only recently, however, has science recognized people will become grouchy anytime their chickens quit laying eggs.

The relationship between short days, fewer eggs, and grouchy people was well-known when I was a kid. Kids fed the chickens in those days, and winter always meant fewer eggs and grouchy people, especially when they found out you didn't take time to thaw the waterers.

Even the old excuse, "It's a darn poor chicken that can't break through a couple of inches of ice," couldn't get us off the hook in that situation.

In addition to shorter days and fewer eggs, I think exercise plays a role in how a person feels during the winter. It's doubtful that scientists will back me up on this — because I just made the whole thing up this morning, but it makes sense to me. If a person doesn't get enough exercise his pituitary gland regresses, and he becomes grouchy.

Everyone has a favorite way to exercise during bad weather, but dragging hay bales across a muddy barnlot remains one of my favorites. Nobody ever got fat dragging hay bales through mud and snow. The fat guys sank down and soon disappeared.

These activities aren't available to everyone, however. A fellow dragging a hay bale gets some nasty looks on suburban sidewalks, so he has to take up something more respectable like jogging.

The trend in modern exercise is to buy a work-out video to help keep in shape during bad weather. There's something about buying an exercise tape, plugging it into the VCR and watching other people sweat that makes a person feel good regardless of what's going on outside. Physicians say these videos accomplish even more if the purchaser actually does some exercises.

I used to scoff at work-out tapes when they were made by people like Richard Simmons. Richard always gave me the feeling he wouldn't drag a bale of hay if his life and forty cows depended on it.

But now tapes are made by working people and athletes, people like Cher. That's the main point in buying a video in my opinion. Get one that's done by someone you can identify with.

The second thing to remember when starting an exercise program is to set realistic goals. Don't expect to create muscles or lose weight all at once, especially if you don't do the exercises.

Work-out enthusiasts say losing weight is not a good objective, anyway. Improving muscle tone is a better goal. There's no way to measure that.

Sure, I Can Hear

I don't know about you, but I'm tired of sales calls. I don't mind calls from someone I do business with; but folks who go through the phone book, calling up everyone, are a pain in the neck.

Last week I got a call from a hearing-aid company. They wanted to give me a hearing test. "Our representative will be in your area next week and would be happy to stop by for a free hearing examination," they told me.

"What?" I said. "You'll have to speak up. I can't hear a thing you're saying."

"We want to check your hearing!" the caller shouted.

"No, my paint isn't smearing," I told her. "We just got new siding and the roof is fine, too."

Then, I hung up. "That should stop them for awhile," I thought. Who do they think they're kidding, calling-up folks and suggesting hearing exams?

If they want to give hearing exams, they should be sending letters. If they want to give eye exams, then call us on the phone. You can't call a deaf person and set up an appointment!

I figure the hearing-aid people are trying to sell us something we don't need. That's why nobody calls to offer free eye exams. (They send letters for those.)

Can you imagine this guy coming to my house to check my hearing? He probably has some fancy equipment — or a watch that doesn't tick, to convince me I need a hearing-aid.

These telemarketers remind me of the old-time vacuum sweeper salesmen; the ones who would throw dirt all over your rug, and then try to prove how good their vacuum was.

The old-fashioned salesmen had to watch their step, though. Readers may have heard about the young sweeper salesman who arrived at a remote farmhouse with his vacuum and a bag of shop-sweepings.

This farm was way out in the boonies, but the lady of the house let him in, anyway. Peddlers were just part of the environment in those days, and a sweeper salesman was still kind of a novelty.

"Our vacuum is guaranteed to out-perform anything you have ever used, or you get your money back," the salesman began. "This is our top-of-the-line, commercial model, with 14 attachments and the extra long cord."

Then, he tossed his bag of dirt all over the cream-colored carpet, and proceeded to unravel his sweeper cord.

"Don't you worry about your carpet for one minute," he said, searching for an electrical outlet. "If this vacuum doesn't clean this dirt up in less than 30 seconds. I'll lick it up myself."

"Well, I sure hope you skipped breakfast," she said. "Cause we're four miles from electricity, and that's a brand new rug you'll be eating from."

Politics Explained

I don't know what it takes to run for President, but it isn't much, I can tell you that. At last count there were 22 Republicans, 21 Democrats, and a couple of Libertarians signed up for the presidential primary in New Hampshire.

Everyone agrees most of these folks don't have a snowball's chance, but why are they running? That's the big question.

I think we need to think back a generation or two if we want to understand the political process in this country. We should harken back to the farm belt — where candidates were born and campaigns were launched 40 years ago. Then, we can better comprehend why folks will run for office with no hope what-so-ever of winning.

I remember as a kid sitting on the tractor seat and listening to farmers talk about politics and elections of all kinds. This was spring, and we were planting corn and soybeans. Everyone was working as fast as they could to get the crop in the ground.

Well, almost everybody. Our community always had a

couple of guys who didn't worry much about planting season, or milking time, or getting their hay baled. They didn't like farming, anyway, as far as we could tell.

So, during planting season, these fellows would climb over the fence and lean on our tractors — while they talked about foreign aid and the problems with Congress.

This was planting season, for gosh sakes! The busiest day of the year. Nobody had time to talk.

So, finally someone would say, "You know what, Frank (Jim or whoever), maybe you should run for Congress." Everybody knew this wasn't the right thing to do, but getting this fellow off your tractor wheel was priority number "1" at that time of year.

That's all it took, one little comment. Before you could say "scat" we had posters on the fences, speeches at the Grange, and somebody would organize one of those big, $4.00-a-plate dinners to help send this man off to Washington, D.C.

Some of them got elected, and we got a lot of corn planted; but now the chickens have come home to roost. Now, we have 45 candidates for the New Hampshire primary. How could this happen?

I think it's pretty clear. These folks were just sitting around the house one day, pestering their wives (or husbands), when the spouse said, "You know what, Richard (or Lucy or whoever), maybe you should run for President."

The rest is history. New Hampshire will have its primary, the media will have a heyday, and we can all watch it on television if we wish.

Just remember, though, when the TV cameras scan the crowd, and we see all those women with big smiles on their faces, those are the candidates' wives. They are so happy to get these guys out of the house, they can barely control themselves.

What'll You Have?

I hate shopping in the city. I'd rather stop at a little store in town than wander through shopping malls, trying to remember where I parked the car.

I don't look at shopping as recreation the way some people do. When I go shopping it's because I've been forced into it, and I don't fool around.

I figure my travel at $.25 per mile, plus parking, and lunch. My time has to be worth something, too.

If I drive 100 miles, charge my time at $5 per hour, and pay $8 for lunch and parking, I figure I need $70 worth of bargains just to pay for the shopping trip.

I remember the mental anguish of driving through traffic, too. It's like a friend said, "It seems strange that folks drive into the city, and instead of slowing down, they speed up!"

I'm not opposed to buying things out of town when necessary, but I can't feature driving 100 miles and spending half a day to save $10.

The local merchants deserve a shot at our business, too. They have to put up with us every time we need a whatchamacallit or a thingamajig, and there's no reason to ignore them when we need something bigger.

I'd rather shop in small towns, anyway. I know where to find the stores, and the clerks can tell you whether they have what you're looking for.

If the little store doesn't have it, they'll tell you where to get it. If nobody has it, we can assume folks around here don't need it, anyway.

A really good country clerk will not only talk you out of items they don't have, but make you feel kind of bad about asking for them.

I suppose this could be carried too far. My brother-in-law likes to eat in a restaurant near his home in Florida where the owner tells the customer what he's having for lunch.

Larry says a person goes into this restaurant and orders a French-dip sandwich and the owner says, "You don't want that. What you want is a hamburger with the works." So the customer says, "Okay, I guess I'll have a hamburger."

A friend told me of a similar place in Montana, where he and several other hunters stopped for breakfast one morning. The old guy who ran the place was both cook and waiter.

Some of the hunters ordered pancakes and eggs. Others wanted ham, bacon, hash browns, French toast, western omelets. The old fellow wrote everything down on his little pad and returned to the kitchen.

When their orders arrived, everyone got pancakes and eggs. Maybe that's all the old-timer knew how to cook? Or maybe that's all he had?

Nobody asked any questions, though. These fellows knew the cardinal rule of the country cafe: When you don't know what's going on, you just shut up and eat.

Watch Out For Looneys

One of the moms was talking to herself. “All I need is one more entry or one more kid, and I’ll be totally out of my mind! When this fair comes around again I hope someone breaks my arm so I don’t enter anything,” she said.

This woman is typical of the thousands who suffer from the compulsion to exhibit livestock at county fairs around the country. Like compulsive shoppers, car washers, or cat fanciers, these folks just don’t know when to quit.

Rural psychologists say those who suffer from “Livestock Ownership Obligations Nearly Every Year” (LOONEY) are nothing new, but their numbers are increasing. A common treatment for the disease is to lie down on a bale of hay; and by the time the fair is over, you’ll probably feel better.

Scientists say LOONEY sufferers will respond to treatment, but their tendency to hang out with other livestock exhibitors makes diagnosis difficult. It’s hard to spot a LOONEY when everyone around them is as crazy as they are.

I believe Livestock Ownership Obligations Nearly Every Year is inherited, but environment plays a strong part.

Some psychologists argue that symptoms, such as manure on your Levis, can't be inherited; but when your father has the same thing, the evidence is pretty clear to me.

A typical LOONEY goes through year after year of attending fairs and livestock shows, with little hope of quitting as long as there are children and animals around the house. Some blame the kids, and may quit having them (as a defensive response).

Help is available, however, from 4-H clubs dedicated to people who exhibit livestock. 4-H clubs provide a safe environment where parents of young livestock owners can stand up and talk about things without fear of ridicule.

I have stood up in such meetings and described what the sheep did today — and suffered only muffled laughter as a result.

By attending meetings, the compulsive livestock owner can learn the many techniques for feeding animals. 4-H meetings help a person understand why it takes three bottles of soap to wash a pig: One bottle is poured on the pig, one falls over and runs down the gutter, and the third is eaten by the pig.

A parent also learns the hazards of giving too much assistance and advice. When something goes wrong, the kids will claim, "My dad said . . ."

Many years ago I tried to help my daughter clip her lamb. Laura was having trouble blending the long wool on the shoulder into closely shorn wool on the legs.

"Here, let me show you how to do that," I said. About the second pass with the clippers I nicked a piece of skin on the lamb's shank, and the cut began to bleed.

"You cut my lamb! You cut my lamb!" Laura shouted.

"Don't you tell anyone I cut your lamb," I warned. "If you do, I'll make you pay for your feed."

The Family Farm

Everyone wants to save the family farm. Farm organizations, environmental groups, and people like me all want to save the homestead. This is fine. Agriculture is the backbone of America, and anything that helps farmers benefits us all.

I do have a question, though: After we save the family farm, what are we going to do with it?

This may sound strange, but anyone who has purchased a family farm knows what I'm talking about. You can buy the land, and the cows, and all of the machinery, but where can you get the family to do the work?

I'm surely not going to crawl out of bed at 4:00 A.M. to milk 30 cows, slop the hogs, and drive a 1950 John Deere from dawn 'til dark. Anyone who thinks I am has been smoking the corn silks again.

That's the problem with our romantic concept of the family farm. It's a bit out of date.

I grew up on a farm, and I've seen things change. The farm was a wonderful place to live when I was a kid, but we didn't expect to have all of the things people now consider essential.

The town kids thought we were rich because we lived in a big farm house. Just like we think today's farmers are rich because they drive a big tractor.

One of my brothers bought Dad's cows and machinery when I was in high school. He later bought the entire farm. I lit out for college at the first opportunity.

Over the years my brother has purchased and leased more land, maintained modern equipment, and insisted on making a decent living like the rest of us.

How's that for gratitude? We want him to preserve the place so the rest of us can hunt squirrels, but he goes and turns the whole thing into a business!

Farmers have been doing this all over the country. They have adopted technology and used their management ability to become larger and more efficient. Many have incorporated, like other businesses.

Some folks think farmers shouldn't be allowed these options. They believe farming more land turns these places into "megafarms," and incorporation makes them "huge corporate farms," as described by television commentators.

That's baloney. Why should farmers have to milk the same 40 cows for the rest of their lives?

When I read about "the nation's largest farms" grossing over $100,000 a year, I think of my own business — and remember that gross income is a long way from net. All I have to maintain is a couple of computers. A farmer has expenses that would scare the rest of us to death.

Those who want to save the family farm will have to decide what we want to preserve. The USDA agricultural census defines a farm as a place with gross sales of more than $1,000 worth of agricultural produce in one year.

If we plan to save all of those, we had better pack a lunch.

Censored Again

Readers with long memories may recall the last time I wrote about censorship. It was the mid-'80s, and the Supreme Court had just ruled against the student newspaper staff in Hazelwood, Missouri — and in favor of the school board and administration.

The high school principal in Hazelwood was accused of deleting certain stories from the school paper, and the students took their case all the way to the Supreme Court, claiming this was a violation of their constitutional rights and a clear case of censorship.

The Court ruled otherwise, saying the principal acted as publisher of the student news. The guys in robes said the publisher takes the risks, and therefore, calls the shots.

I seized this concept like an owl catches mice — agreeing profusely with the Supreme Court. I wrote that determining what to print is not censorship: It's decision-making. Publishers do this every day, buying things like my column or tossing them aside according to their needs, budget, or sense of humor.

I got that column back from a newspaper in Missouri, along with a deduction from my check. The publisher said the subject was too controversial, so he couldn't use it.

This proved my point, of course; and wouldn't have been so bad, but the man docked my check for more than he normally paid for a column! This showed me how upset people can get about censorship.

Much of this tooth-gnashing results from a confusion of terms, in my opinion. We have become so defensive about censorship that we've lost the meaning of the word.

My dictionary defines censorship as "The institution, system, or practice of censoring." Censoring is "to examine in order to delete anything considered objectionable."

Censorship is a systematic process of banning ideas or eliminating things considered objectionable. The everyday chore of buying materials and making decisions in schools and libraries is not generally censorship.

I publish a few books, to cite a personal example, and thousands of purchasers will attest they aren't bad reading. People buy them, and even give them as gifts.

Many libraries don't purchase my books, however. Maybe they don't like them, or perhaps these books aren't objectionable enough. If they were more offensive, some would feel compelled to buy them to avoid the specter of censorship.

I made sure our local library got some — by donating a copy of each title. The library system bought a few, also.

I know my books are out there somewhere, but I've never seen a copy in our library. That's because they're on the bookmobile, bouncing along the lonesome roads of the hinterlands. Out in the boonies, where life is simple and all of the readers are ahead of their age group.

Is this censorship? Should libraries be required to buy my books, or bring them back to town where city people can read them?

Of course not! Library officials don't have to purchase everything published, and they can put the books anywhere they want.

That's not censorship. It's decision-making and budgeting — part of the everyday operation.

Besides, some books are just naturals for the bookmobile. Many should be up front where everyone can find them. A few should go in the back — under the spare tire.

Country Salesmen

There's never a shortage of good salesmen in a rural community. I don't know what causes it, but there's something about living in the country that gives a person an edge when it comes to selling.

You'll find them at the machinery dealers, real estate offices, and the appliance stores. People who can peddle ice to an Eskimo and then sell him a new cooler to put it in.

Retired farmers are especially good at this. They've been selling things to each other for so long, they know exactly what to say and when to say it.

I learned years ago some of the country's best salesmen don't even know how good they are. They're just nice people who try to give you an honest deal.

My neighbor, Lynn, is a good example. Like most of the great ones, Lynn isn't even a salesman. He's a contractor, but he would make a fine salesman if he ever decides to change careers.

I discovered Lynn's sales ability when I bought his boat a few weeks ago. At least I think it was his boat. He might have several more parked behind the barn for all I know.

Never mind that I already had a boat — and needed another like a big hole in the head. This boat was in excellent shape and just the right size for the kind of fishing I always planned to do someday. I couldn't pass it up!

Besides, Lynn is an honest guy. He's the kind of person I want to deal with when buying a used boat. (A boating expert like me can't be too careful, you know.)

Of course I checked the boat out and made sure there weren't any slaves in the galley or bees in the ballast or anything like that. Then, I commented what great shape this craft was in for its age.

"It has always been under cover," Lynn said, "I bought the boat out of a barn, and I've always kept it covered and in the barn after I got it."

"That's what I need to do one of these days," I told him. "I need to build a storage building for boats and vehicles. We really don't have a good place to put them."

That's when I learned what a great salesman my neighbor is. By the time I was done with this deal, I not only owned the boat, I had Lynn building me a barn to put it in!

Then, as I was leaving Lynn's place with the boat we got to talking about those big, flightless birds he raises. Emus, I think they're called.

A lot of folks are getting into raising exotic birds, like emus and ostriches. From what I've heard, a couple of emus should lay enough high-priced eggs to help me pay for my new barn in a hurry.

I would need a chain-link fence for the birds, of course, but Lynn could probably build that while he's doing the barn.

I've been planning to stop by and talk with him about it; but my wife says I had better stay away from that man if I know what's good for me.

What Now Brown Cow?

A recent visit to a modern dairy barn reminded me of how far we have progressed in milk production. Management and efficiency are the key words these days, and most dairymen even hire someone else to do the milking.

When I was a kid nobody hired people to milk cows. That was like hiring someone to wash your dishes — the ultimate self-indulgence.

Besides, a person couldn't milk someone else's cows in those days. You had to know the cows on a first name basis or they would kick the snot out of you. Even if you were lucky enough to survive what the cows could dish-out, the equipment would finish you off.

Our milking was done in stanchions where a guy had to sidle up next to a cow and convince her he was pretty much harmless before he could even think about putting the milker on her. In those days we used the old Surge milkers that hung from a strap over the cow's back.

The person doing the milking had to squeeze in between two cows and hang the belt over the one to be milked, while trying to convince the cow behind him she would be hamburger if she so much as lifted a leg. Then he would hang the milker on the belt, attach the cups to the udder, and adjust the belt for that particular cow.

It worked remarkably well for most cows, but there were always exceptions. The exception I remember best was an old, brown cow named Susie.

Susie had a trace of Ayrshire blood in her, giving her those big, brown eyes with an inordinate amount of white showing around the edges. Susie always looked frightened, and she had good reason: We threatened to kill her nearly every day.

When we opened the milking-barn door, Susie would jump through it like a lion bounding through a hoop, and then she would slide about halfway down the concrete alley behind the stanchions. By the time she calmed down and got into a stanchion, that cow was panic stricken. It was like she had never been milked before.

You would think an animal that had entered the barn twice-a-day for four years could find a stanchion without getting lost, but Susie never perfected it. She would run to the other end of the aisle and whirl around before the other cows got halfway into the barn. Then she would jam her head between the stanchion and the frame holding it, and remain stuck until someone belted her in the nose to back her out.

This was one of those cows we had to use the kickers on. For those who haven't seen kickers, they were made of two pieces of steel, shaped to fit around a cow's hocks. The two leg attachments were held together by a chain, which could be adjusted to hold the cow's hocks together so she couldn't lift a foot to kick you.

These contraptions worked fine until a cow figured out how to kick with both feet, and then you had a bovine jackass on your hands.

When I enter a modern dairy I'm always amazed that a dairyman works all his life for a nice milking parlor and some civilized equipment, and then he hires someone else to do the milking. Somehow it just doesn't seem fair.

Help For The Humor Impaired

The hardest thing about writing a news column is answering questions from readers. Even simple queries like, "How long does it take to write a column?" never seem to have an easy answer.

Does a column take a couple of hours, or a couple of days? Or a couple of years? I don't know. I'm not sure I've ever finished one!

When I first started writing, people would ask, "Do you write that column yourself?"

"What do they mean by that?" I wondered. Do they think I'm too dumb to write this stuff, or too smart to write it? It's a no-win situation as far as I can tell.

The hardest question of all is, "How did you get started writing?" I've mulled that one around for years, and my mind always skips back to the very early years of grade school.

You have to understand I grew up in the era before creative writing was taught, or even encouraged, in the lower grades. Students who tried to be creative, or refused to color between the lines, generally wound up in the boiler room talking with the janitor.

My old school wasn't the most progressive — even then, so my early writing was terse and to the point.

"Roger is sic today. Probbly has the flew. Signed, Dad." That kind of stuff.

As I advanced through the grades, my teachers began comparing my writing with others. "This reminds me of Steinbeck," Mrs. Arbuck would say. "You and Bobby Steinbeck are staying after school until we find out who's copying from whom."

Soon my teachers were comparing my writing to that of my sister, then my older brother, and finally they decided they didn't care where I was getting it — as long as it wasn't hurting anyone else.

By the time I reached junior high my sense of humor had blossomed, flowered, ripened (take your pick). That's when I learned humor wasn't taught at my school, either. It seemed to be discouraged, if anything.

If Mrs. Arbuck saw something humorous, she did everything she could to squelch it. Whereas most humorists have people encouraging them, I've had to go it pretty much alone.

When David Letterman was a child, his teachers would say, "Oh, Dave that's so funny! I'll bet your mother is very proud of you." That's why he grew up to be such a smart aleck.

My teachers didn't see things that way. My teachers were what Garrison Keillor calls "humor impaired."

Mrs. Arbuck in particular was death on young humorists. "You may have thought that was funny, but I certainly didn't," she would say.

"Don't be so hard on yourself," I told her. "Just hang in there, and you'll probably catch on right away next time."

This seemed to cheer her up, but I've always wondered about a woman who grinds her teeth like that when she smiles. It must be hard on the molars, if nothing else.

Now We're Getting Warm

I'm still working on this global warming thing, but I think I'm getting a feel for it. A *New York Times* News Service story provides the hard data I've been looking for.

The *New York Times* story reports British scientists have learned 1995 was the warmest year globally since weather records were begun in 1856. The British say the average temperature in 1995 was 58.7 degrees Fahrenheit.

That's seven hundredths of a degree hotter than it was in 1990, and 1990 was the warmest year since 1866. For some reason 1866 was a hot one, also.

A weather chart accompanying the *New York Times* story shows the average world temperature has hovered around 58 degrees since 1944, the year I was born. This follows closely with my own experience. I don't think I've ever been hotter than when I was born (except for 1995).

Some may question the value of short-term averages and personal observation in predictions such as these, but we have to start somewhere. I became a staunch believer in statistical averaging while completing a research project some years ago. That study showed the average American shaves only one side of its face.

A look back at our global weather shows some clear

trends. Records indicate 1866 was quite hot. Then we went into a cooling trend.

The world got up around 58 degrees for particular years in the late 1800s; then we dropped back to about 57.5 (off and on), until one exceptionally hot year of about 57.8 around 1920. The earth's climate plummeted to 57 degrees for a year or two in the '20s, but folks who were there say it felt much colder than that.

The global climate was hot and cold, hot and cold, hot and cold, until about 1944 — which was another exceptional year, as mentioned earlier. My mother says my average temperature was around 98.6 in 1944.

Now, to the question of global warming and predictions for the future. A quick look at the British data shows the average global temperature has followed a well-defined pattern.

Some years are kind of sultry, but the average of 58 degrees is still darned comfortable. We can't complain about that.

Exceptionally warm years like 1866, the late 1800s, 1944, and 1995 can all be explained by man's activity on the planet, especially in the United States. Nobody else has done anything, as far as I can tell.

The end of the Civil War in the 1860s was a hot time for sure, with all the men returning from the war, and the North's industrial power being converted from munitions to carpet bags.

The late 1800s must have been special, too, with the long dresses, wool underwear, and raccoon coats. Everybody was hot in the 1890s.

How it got so warm in 1995 (and we still had to shovel all that snow) is pretty hard for me to understand. Younger scientists say this just proves global warming causes erratic weather.

I'm no scientist, and my charts may be erratic, but that weather table from the *New York Times* story shows the last fifty years has produced the most consistent global temperatures since records began in 1856.

I can't explain that, either; but I checked again this morning, and my temperature is still around 98.6 degrees. I find that very comforting.

How To Clog Up A Gopher

How do you get rid of gophers? Ask that question of a dozen people and you will get 12 different answers.

When someone asks me how to get rid of gophers, I generally suggest they bury them behind the barn. Sometimes, I say, "Just give them to me, and I'll get rid of them for you."

Then I jump back a couple of feet, just in case these folks don't have a sense of humor.

Moles are easier to control than gophers, of course. They burrow right along the surface of the ground. A person can actually see the earth moving when a mole is working in his hill.

I saw a news report on television a while back in which a determined looking fellow was describing his technique for mole control. The TV crew approached as the man was sitting in his pasture, watching an active mole hill.

This fellow's elbows were braced on his knees, and his nickel-plated .38 rested securely between his hands. "When you see the dirt move, you have to shoot straight down the hole. Otherwise you'll miss 'em," he said.

The TV cameras zoomed in on the mole hill and suddenly, ka-boom! "Rats, missed another one," the man said.

This fellow had the dour and disheartened look of a person who has tried everything. The moles had him on the ropes, but he was determined to fight for his pasture.

My wife had a similar look on her face when she trudged in from her flower garden recently. Connie doesn't own a revolver, thank goodness, but she was every bit as mad as the guy on TV.

She had some chewing gum, and was stuffing it into her mouth as fast as she could open the packages. "I've got the right kind now," she said. "Juicy Fruit. They say it has to be Juicy Fruit."

"Oh, so that's it," I said. "You chew up some gum and put it in the gopher burrows. Then, the gophers get into the habit of chewing gum and their teeth fall out; so they can't hurt your plants."

"Several people told me this works," she said. "The gophers eat the gum and it clogs up their digestive system. The bad part is I get sick chewing up all this gum."

"Why not take it into school and let the kids chew it," I suggested. "Or ask the janitors to save the stuff they find under the desks."

Then, I jumped back a few feet. Just a reflex, I guess.

I've never had much confidence in alternative methods of gopher control. The research I've seen says you can trap them or you can poison them, but no way can you discourage them. A gopher is an eternal optimist.

I'll never forget the summer I purged my garden of gophers by setting traps. I didn't catch anything, but they all moved to my wife's flower beds and haven't bothered me since.

Family Stories

Every family has it's stories, handed down through the generations like an old piece of furniture. Like the furniture, these tales have been sanded and varnished, but the framework remains intact.

Many family stories are remnants of the days when folks sat on the porch and visited. Telling stories was an art form before TV destroyed western civilization as we knew it.

My dad and uncles were famous for stories. They would sit on the porch for hours, staring into the darkness and retelling an old yarn most of us had heard dozens of times.

Nobody objected to hearing these fables retold, though, because you never really heard the same story twice. Something new was added with each telling until the story seemed to have a life of its own. Accuracy is irrelevant to a good story-teller.

Dad would tell about the time a young neighbor slid his bicycle on the gravel road and rolled elbows over teakettle through the shrubbery that surrounded Uncle Dale's front yard. When the young cyclist slid to a stop near the flower bed,

Uncle Dale asked, "Where are you going in such a hurry?"

"Well, I *was* going to visit my sister in Jackson Center!" the young man exclaimed.

Everyone would laugh at this, and then Uncle Willis would tell about the great squirrel migration.

It seems one of our pioneer ancestors was driving his wagon down the road one day, when he suddenly found himself surrounded by thousands of squirrels. Nobody knew where they came from or where they were going, but squirrels were everywhere.

A little dog in the wagon nearly went crazy. He seemed to think the squirrels had formed a union and were coming to get him.

The dog might have been a fox terrier, or a collie. Sometimes he was a bird dog. One time he was a coon hound.

Each time the story was retold the squirrels ran faster, the dog barked louder, and every so often there would be a couple of badgers in the herd — just to add some excitement.

I've often wondered what that tale sounded like the first time it was conveyed. It might have been three squirrels and a chipmunk for all I know.

My dad and uncles are gone now, and most of the old stories went with them. Every family says they need to write these things down, but few of us do.

Recently though, I've learned there might be a better way. Many Native American tribes have what they call an "oral history," sort of an unwritten record that recounts events from the past.

These verbal histories are said to go back hundreds and thousands of years. They sometimes take precedence over more recent written records in a court of law.

I wish my family had thought of that. If we could retell those old stories for a few more generations I think we could have us some real doozies.

Dear Miss Understanding:

I have always wanted to be a "question and answer" columnist: The kind that receives questions in the mail and has an answer for everything.

I could call myself "Miss Understanding," or something like that.

This isn't as easy as it sounds. Answers are like apples: They will rot if allowed to sit around until the right question comes along.

In addition to keeping the answers fresh, the advice columnist has to make sure each question is legitimate — and not the product of a twisted sense of humor.

A good example is a letter that appeared in a column featuring homemaking tips. The letter writer offered the following hint: "To clean stubborn stains from the toilet bowl, pour 1/4 cup of lemon juice into the bowl and leave overnight."

This sounds innocent enough, but we can see it could be a waste of time and money. Readers who tried it finally realized the lemon juice works just as well if you stay at home.

Food writers, especially, have to watch how they say things. The special shorthand used in recipes is so vulnerable to confusion.

A good example is the cookbook author who published her recipe for "Sautéed Chicken Breasts." The recipe went along fine until the point where it instructed cooks to, "Spoon salad dressing over each breast."

Kitchen testing confirmed what readers had been saying: Male cooks generally completed this recipe successfully, but women had a tendency to give up at this point.

A more personal example is a letter I received recently from a man who wants to get started farming. This fellow is nearing retirement and hopes to buy a hobby farm with his extra cash.

This may be a reasonable request for information, but it has all the earmarks of a hoax. My experience would suggest getting started farming is no problem. Getting stopped is the hard part.

By the time a person buys all the equipment needed to get started, he has to continue farming to keep the creditors at bay. There's no way out.

Everyone who buys a few acres goes through the same chain of thought. First one wonders what can be grown to help pay the taxes. Then, we consider the machinery needed for this type of enterprise. Finally, the small landholder realizes he'd better just pay his taxes and forget the farming.

I suppose that's why I'll never be a question and answer columnist: I'm too blunt.

When someone asks about hobby farming, I'm likely to suggest he spoon some salad dressing over his head and leave overnight. By the time he returns, his thinking should have cleared considerably.

Checkmate

The media is surely making a big deal out of the Bobby Fischer — Boris Spassky chess match. First we read about the $5 million prize money, and now the papers are printing the moves from each game, as if the whole country is on the edge of our chairs

I find it disgraceful that two grown men would sit down to play chess as if their lives (and $5 million) depended upon this one little match. We played for more than that when I was a kid, and nobody blinked an eye.

Chess is a kid's game, meant to be played on a rainy day — when you have friends over, and everybody's tired of lassoing the cat. Not something for grown men to be fussing about.

My younger brother, Merlin, was the chess expert in our family. Merlin was eight years old when we got the chess set, and he would play for any amount you wished to name.

I'd walk into the house and say, "Okay, Merlin, this game's for $5 million. And he'd say, "Let's make it $10 million, so you won't be wasting my time."

If I won, we'd go double-or-nothing until Merlin won. It was like trading two $4,000 dogs for an $8,000 dog — or boxing professionally.

But Merlin never lost. He had the rule book, and being the youngest, generally got his way on rules interpretations.

Chess enthusiasts would tell us the object is to threaten your opponent's king in such a way that the king cannot escape capture. When the king is threatened, the aggressor says, "Check." Then, his opponent tries to find some way to get his king out of the fix he's in. If the king can't escape, we have "Checkmate," and the game is over.

Merlin played the game as if it were checkers: He shouted "Checkmate!" and took your king without warning (and often without explanation). There was none of this checking and fooling around. One minute the king was alive, and the next he was dead.

After playing Merlin I'd take on Spassky any day, but I'd have to brush up my terminology. My brothers and I played for years with a king and queen, eight little guys, two horses, some bishops, and two crooks.

That would be a match worth watching: Pond Vs. Spassky. We might schedule it for neutral territory, such as Spassky's living room. It would be raining, so we wouldn't have to bale hay or work in the garden.

Spassky's mother would offer us cookies, and I'd say, "No thanks, I just ate. My mother said not to ask for food. I'm not supposed to eat sweet stuff. Boy, these are good cookies." (Farm kids refuse everything three times before they eat it.)

Then the match begins. Pond opens with one of his little guys, and Spassky counters with his horse. Pond moves his king and a crook at the same time.

"You can't do that!" Spassky says.

"Merlin does it. He calls it castling queen side," I tell him.

"Checkmate!" Bam! I knock Spassky's king off the board.

He runs to the kitchen yelling, "Roger's cheating! Roger's cheating!"

"Now, Boris," Mrs. Spassky says. "You'd better learn how to play with your friends, or we'll have to take the chessboard and give it to the Salvation Army."

It's Only Money

Every so often my wife and I get into a discussion about money. Not one of those "to spend or not to spend" feuds so familiar to marriage counselors — just a nice philosophical talk.

We don't always agree, of course. I'm a conservative when it comes to spending and investing, and my wife is more liberal in her financial beliefs.

A tin can in the back yard is a reliable savings vehicle, as far as I'm concerned, while Connie believes mutual funds will keep going up as long as the fund manager doesn't run off with the Gypsies.

She's been right so far. There just aren't as many Gypsies as there used to be.

One thing we agree on is that money is a lot more fun if you enjoy spending it. Many times a person has to spend it, anyway, so he might as well enjoy it.

We have friends who spend more than they should, and others who become physically ill when they have to buy something that isn't "on sale." I've been guilty of both.

Those who don't enjoy spending generally have more in the long run, but there's no sense being miserable when you're supposed to be having a good time.

My best lesson in buying things was a trip to Europe some years ago. We didn't spend a lot by today's standards, but the foreign money was the interesting part for me.

We got some pounds in London, francs in Paris, and funny little coins in Germany. Nobody knew how to count these things, so we just handed them over to clerks, waiters, and cab drivers, and took our chances.

A waiter would hold out his hand, and we'd give him a wad of funny money. Then, he would count it out and give back whatever he didn't need.

It's amazing how much fun you can have when you don't know what it's costing.

On the opposite side of the coin, I've been known to make myself miserable trying to save 50 cents on parking when I've already spent $40 getting into town.

Differing philosophies about life and money remind me of a little poem I've seen several times over the years. It goes something like this:

There was a very cautious man
Who never laughed or played
He never risked, he never tried
He never sang or prayed
And when one day he passed away
His insurance was denied
They claimed he never really lived
So how could he have died!?

Caught Knapping

What should I do with all these antlers? That's the question of the day.

Thirty years of deer hunting has borne fruit (or horns), so to speak, and now I'm up to my hocks in headgear. I've got antlers in the basement, antlers in the barn, and horns scattered around the yard.

These aren't exactly trophies, of course, but I can't seem to throw any of them away. Someday I'll probably grind them up and add them to my soup; but for now they're just a bit of a nuisance.

I know folks will say I could sell the antlers, or send them to the Orient where folks know what to do with them; but I don't expect to get rich selling deer horns. I'll probably just keep moving them around each time I have to clean out the basement.

That's why my ears perked up, when my brother-in-law asked if he could have an antler to make some tools. Charley has been frequenting rock shops and purchased a book on the art of knapping. He needed a blunt object for whacking pieces off a rock.

"This book shows how to make arrow heads and knives from certain kinds of rocks," Charley said. "The author says a deer antler makes one of the best tools for chipping slivers off a rock."

I should explain that Charley and I are good friends, but different personalities. Charley designs computer software and thinks like an engineer. He likes to read and learn new things.

He even reads instructions. Charley won't open a can of soup without checking the calories per serving, grams of fat, and instructions for recycling the can.

I write for a living and think like a sheepherder. I don't read directions until I've tried everything else. I look at the photo on a soup can and say, "This looks good. Let's eat it and see what it is."

You can imagine our conversation when Charley said he needed a deer antler to chip away at some rocks. My face registered my chagrin.

"You're certainly welcome to an antler," I said, "But there must be easier ways to get an arrow head. Sitting in front of a cave, pounding on rocks with a deer horn is not my idea of a good time."

"It's called knapping," Charley said. "People do it as a hobby. I thought it looked interesting."

I finally gave Charley an antler and held my tongue about his new hobby. I could have made jokes about being caught knapping or getting the point, but I didn't.

Then, this week, I saw a newspaper feature about a man who makes some very interesting knives by pounding on a piece of rock with a blunt object. He sells them at shows for $400 to $700 each!

Maybe I was a bit cynical about Charley's new hobby. I probably should send him some rocks and some antlers and encourage him to chip away.

You can bet I'll include instructions, too:

Step 1 — Hit rock with antler.

Step 2 — Repeat Step 1.

Step 3 — Send knives to brother-in-law.

One Cow Dog And Two Bales Of Hay

We read a lot about the decline in agricultural employment and the need to diversify rural economies. Many sociologists believe top priority should be given to creating off-farm jobs for farmers, and then second or third jobs for their wives.

I couldn't agree more, and hope to have my new business up and running within the next few weeks. My company will be called "Country Consultants," and will employ retired farmers and farm women to give advice to city dwellers moving into rural areas.

The concept is similar to a business in California that gives seminars on how to move to Oregon and Washington. The California outfit provides prospective immigrants with information on housing, jobs, and lifestyles in various parts of the Northwest.

My company will go a step further and tell folks how to act once they get there. This may seem trivial to some readers, but subtle differences between urban and rural attitudes put newcomers at a serious disadvantage.

We could take, for example, the folks who moved to a

small rural community and wanted to paint a horse on the side of their pickup. The new residents told their neighbors, "Now that we have a ranch and some horses, we're thinking about painting the head of a horse on our truck."

The neighbors said, "Oh, good heavens, no! You don't want the picture of a horse on your truck. Around here, you just need a cow dog in the front and two bales of hay in the back."

That's good advice. It's okay for long-time residents to paint a horse on their truck, because everyone already knows these people; but this is deadly for a newcomer. Horses are utilitarian beasts in farm and ranching areas and any attempt to glorify them is a major faux pas (pronounced "fox paws").

That's the kind of advice Country Consultants hopes to provide: Subtle little things — so obvious to older residents we don't even think about them anymore.

New residents may wonder, "Why two bales of hay? Why not three bales, or one? What kind of hay? Why a cow dog, instead of a German shepherd?" Old-timers know these things, but someone has to tell the new people.

Let's start with the hay. Two bales is correct. Three is considered showing-off; and a person with only one bale looks like he forgot the other one. (I know it's subtle, but we have to pay attention.)

What kind of hay? You surely can't drive around with two bales of nice, leafy alfalfa. Anybody who can afford that kind of hay obviously didn't grow up around here.

Get yourself some old, stemmy grass hay; or have your neighbor bale up some sticks this summer. Chances are he already has some in the barn he would be happy to sell you.

Where can you get a cow dog? Just go to the local pound and walk through the kennels. Any dog with pointy ears and beady, little eyes is probably a cow dog according to his owner.

Why is the pound full of cow dogs? They all answer to the same name. That's the main reason.

The dog warden just drives around yelling, "Git in the pickup! You #$%*& @#& of a $#*@#*!"and he's got half the cow dogs in the county, slick as a whistle.

A Slip Of The Tongue

I grew up in a large family. That may not mean much to some folks, but those who were reared in similar circum stances will know what I mean.

Farm families, such as ours, ate most of their meals together, and much of this time was spent joking and kidding around. Learning how to take it, and how to dish it out was part of growing up.

Our dinner conversations were good, wholesome fun for the most part, but a simple request to "pass the potatoes" might have turned nasty if Mother and Dad hadn't kept a lid on things.

You could tell the joking was over when my older brother would say, "How would you like to pick yourself up out of the corner?"

I credit those dinner-time debates for my tendency to speak quickly and my uncanny instinct for saying the wrong thing — to the wrong person — at the wrong time.

Just recently, for example, I was talking with my wife's aunt, who lives in Columbus, Ohio. Aunt Annie was telling me the airlines have lowered their fares to the point where a person can fly from Columbus to Chicago for $45, round-trip.

"People are flying up there, just to spend the day," she exclaimed. "Can you imagine, flying to Chicago for $45!?"

"No, I can't," I said. "They'd have to give me a lot more than $45 to get me to go to Chicago; and that goes for Columbus, too, now that I think about it."

I was going to tell her the old joke about an expense paid trip to Kansas, when I realized I might have said too much, already.

Readers may recall the infamous contest that offered the third place winner a two-week, expense paid trip to Kansas. The second place winner got a one-week holiday in Kansas, and the first place winner didn't have to go to Kansas at all. (See what I mean? Now, I've made all the people from Kansas mad!)

A few days after our air fare conversation, Aunt Annie was telling me about her college experience back in the 1940's. "I was going to Muskingum College, when I saw all the big money to be made in Columbus. So I quit college and went to work," she said. "That was the dumbest thing I ever did. I should have stayed and finished my degree."

"How long were you in college?" I asked.

"One quarter," she said.

"Well, at least you didn't quit at the last minute," I told her.

I slipped up again this summer when I asked a teacher if she was ready for school to start. I don't know how often teachers hear that question, but their reaction is just like cold water hitting a hot stove.

It's a good thing this woman is/was a friend of mine. I certainly wouldn't want a stranger talking to me that way.

It's In The Genes

I don't know what they teach at universities these days, but I'm sure it's worthwhile. I went to college at a time when a kid could enroll in the College of Agriculture and study things like crops and livestock. You can't do that anymore.

Today, a student matriculates into the College of Bio-Diversity, Human Environments, and Terrestrial Investigations. Then, this youngster studies something like "Biological and Societal Implications of Agronomic and Mammalian Endeavors."

It's still crops and livestock, but they don't call it that. Colleges and departments have changed their names and titles so many times in the last 30 years, I can't tell an agronomist from a Greek mythologist anymore.

I was talking with a young friend recently, when the conversation turned to his college major. "What are you studying?" I asked.

"It's called Bio-Systems Engineering," he said (without blinking an eye).

"Huh?" I said. "Now you're trying to confuse me. What

do people in your major actually do?"

"We manage the environment for a particular crop, or in an orchard, for example; so the plant or tree gets the right amount of water — and other elements it needs for optimum production," he told me.

"You're not talking about irrigation management?" I asked.

"Well, partly, but the goal is to manage the whole environment."

"Is pest management part of this, too?" I quizzed.

"We don't get into pests much. We're mostly concerned about delivering water efficiently and having the right growing environment," he explained.

I thought to myself, "That sounds a lot like soil physics and irrigation management," but I didn't want to expose my ignorance any further.

Then, I remembered my young friend's father graduated from the same university nearly thirty years ago. He studied soil physics and irrigation management, among other things.

That clears up the whole situation, as far as I'm concerned. I've watched a lot of kids grow up over the years, and I've learned a few things.

Young people can be baffling for older generations. They speak a different language, listen to horrible music, and fail to show up for dinner.

Young men are especially confusing. How can they stay out so late, sleep on the floor, and drive cars without any gasoline?

Whatever these kids do, though, I've found a good way to understand most of it.

When a young fellow says or does something I just can't comprehend, I try to look back about thirty years; because there's an excellent chance his daddy did exactly the same thing.

Give It To The Lawyers

This is it. My ship has arrived! I knew my old truck would pay-off sooner or later.

I just received the proposed settlement for owners of GMC pickups with "outside the frame" gas tanks. The court for the Parish of Iberville, Louisiana suggests General Motors should reward people with old junkers like mine with a $1,000 certificate toward purchase of a new GMC truck.

I read the same thing in the newspaper several years ago, but it's just now getting through the court system. Those lawyers must be patient little devils.

At any rate, the proposed settlement from General Motors would allow me to take my $1,000 certificate and $30,000 worth of loose change to my nearest GMC dealer and get a new truck. I should be able to find the extra cash under the cushions of my couch.

That's not my only option, however. The proposed settlement says after the first 15 months of the redemption period this certificate would be transferable to anyone who actually has $30,000. Then, this person could use it to knock $250 off the price of a new GMC truck.

Now, before we get too excited about this amazing offer, I should mention there is a lot of court jesting yet to be done. This is merely a proposed settlement that will be under consideration in a court in Louisiana.

Those who wish to be excluded from the class action settlement must write to an address in New Orleans. Those who have objections, but don't want to be excluded, are supposed to write to an address in Plaquemine, Louisiana.

Those who just don't give a darn will do what I'm doing: Nothing. I've seen these class action suits before.

A few readers may recall I once owned a Ford Bronco II that many folks claimed would roll sideways better than either forwards or backwards. As part of that class action suit, I was offered a special deal if I didn't object to the settlement.

The proposed settlement in the Bronco II case suggested each owner receive a free video instructing us how to drive safely with that type of vehicle. Then, we were supposed to get a "Sun-Visor Sticker" to remind us not to spin around corners or spit with the windows up.

We were promised a "hand lantern, with battery," and a Rand McNally road atlas to help us find our way home (or to report our location if we rolled over in a strange place).

Finally the proposed settlement stated, "If the Federal Court and Alabama Supreme Court approve the settlement, these courts will determine what amount (if any) of attorney's fees and reimbursement of costs and expenses should be paid to counsel for the settlement class."

That really got my goat. Those attorneys slaved over this case for years, and now the court might decide not to give them anything for all their efforts!

I wrote about the injustice of the whole thing, and suggested if the court didn't give those lawyers anything, I wanted them to have my lantern and battery.

They must have taken me up on it. It's been two years now, and I haven't even seen the sun-visor sticker.

Tractor Pull

Our society is obsessed with the supernatural. Nearly each week we read about visits from space aliens or some type of strange circles in someone's wheat field.

This fascination with the unknown must be a recent phenomenon. Nobody worried about that kind of stuff when I was a kid. We had bigger things to worry about.

If someone told my father there was a hole in his bean field or a goat on the hen house, he didn't think about extraterrestrials or get excited and call the police. He simply said, "Where are the boys?"

I grew up in a time when the unusual was commonplace, and the ordinary was worthy of suspicion. There were five boys and two girls in my family, and if two of us didn't think of something the other five probably did.

My dad would be combining and notice an acre or so of wheat mashed down into a strange, geometric pattern. He didn't think about aliens, though. He simply looked over the fence at the base paths in the pasture and said, "Must have been a home run."

Dad's reaction was probably similar, but more excited, when he found that huge crater in his corn field one autumn. Nobody knows for sure what he said, because the hole appeared and disappeared without question or fanfare.

An untrained eye might attribute such a crater to the blast from a flying saucer, or an asteroid at the least, but a man with five boys recognized it immediately. This had all the earmarks of a tractor pull.

Readers who haven't seen a tractor pull will have to use their imaginations. A tractor pull is that event at the fairgrounds where a juiced-up tractor is hooked to a heavy sled. Then engines scream, wheels spin, and smoke rolls, while otherwise sane people cheer their favorite machine.

That's how it was that June day when my brothers were supposed to be cultivating corn. Two of the boys had been arguing for months about which tractor was more powerful, and they finally decided to settle it once and for all.

One drove an old Oliver with wide front wheels. The other piloted an Allis Chalmers with narrow wheels and enough power to pull a two-bottom plow on a really good day.

Nobody had a sled, of course, but my brothers found a chain in the truck. So they hooked the old Oliver and Allis together — and turned them loose right in the middle of the corn field! Engines whined, smoke rolled, and tires spun.

A third brother was smart enough to stay out of the whole thing. He became the eye-witness, referee, innocent bystander — depending upon whom you ask. All three have remained silent for more than 40 years, but now admit the main result of their impromptu tractor pull were two huge holes in the corn field.

"How did you fill the holes?" I asked.

"We didn't," they said.

"What did Dad say when he found those holes with the corn picker?" I quizzed.

"Who knows? We surely weren't going to ask him!" they said.

The Garbage Dog

This is it! I have entered the world of modern technology. I have become a composter. (Composter: Person who composts.)

That may not sound like much to some folks, but it is to me. After all these years of uncivilized garbage disposal, I have finally acquired an apparatus for composting.

My composting device is called the "green cone," and consists of a cone (naturally) attached to a plastic laundry basket. One simply places the cone on top of the basket, buries the basket in the ground, and begins inserting garbage.

In a year or so, the composter (person who composts) opens the cone, takes out the garbage and gets rid of it the best way he knows how. Directions for the cone recommend all types of vegetable matter, tea leaves, etc. but no meat for this process.

This sounded great at first; but then I thought, "Wait a minute — what do I do with my meat scraps? How do I turn the compost? Am I really making compost or just getting rid of garbage?"

I was reminded of the old farm dog we kept when I was a kid. Old Brownie operated in much the same way as this "green cone." We could take out a pan of leftovers and yell, "Here Brownie!" And the scraps would be gone before we could get back to the house.

We should have named that dog "Greenie" — he was so environmentally friendly. Brownie took the meat, too. Boy, did he take the meat!

Brownie didn't care if the garbage contained chicken bones, pork chops, or whatever. He could digest anything. He was bred for this kind of work.

Brownie came from a special litter of pups we acquired one spring. His mother was part beagle, and his father was a male dog of some kind; so Brownie wasn't exactly purebred.

There were 10 in the litter — as one would expect from that kind of marriage. One puppy had long ears and looked like a blue-tick hound. Another had the face of a St. Bernard and the body of a rat terrier. A third looked more like a toy poodle, with a shot of greyhound in her.

My brother and I wanted to keep the blue-tick, thinking he would make a good hunting dog; but Dad took the whole bunch to the pound — all except Brownie. I think Dad recognized a good garbage dog when he saw one.

Old Brownie laid around the farm while I went to high school, then college, and was still there when I moved away. I can remember thinking he was the most useless dog in the world.

Now I see entire industries based upon the simple task that old dog performed when I was a kid. It's just another case of a dog being ahead of my time.

If I had Old Brownie and his litter mates today, I could write my own ticket in the garbage disposal industry. Nobody has a good line of garbage dogs anymore. It seems like they've all been bred for show.

How To Ride A Cattle Cycle

This is a great time for economists. I enjoyed a recent article in which one economist was contradicting another about the prospects for farm commodity prices in the coming year. I didn't understand either of them, but it's always fun to see two economists enjoying themselves.

Economists seem to emerge from a deep slumber at this time of year — and stumble around looking for shadows. Some of my favorite reading in January and February consists of economic predictions.

I have never been an economist, but I've become pretty good at predicting commodity prices. If a person watches the forecasts, he will notice certain trends carry over from one year to the next. The following are my predictions for the coming year.

CORN: This crop will be up and down this year. Early planted corn will be up sooner than late planted corn. Both early and late planted crops will fail several times but recover in time for harvest. This will set a record of some kind.

My advice is to hold corn until you just can't stand it any

longer. Then try to sell it for more than your neighbor got.

BEANS: Beans will remain volatile. Consumption should keep pace — despite government warnings about methane and global warming. Watch USDA forecasts to determine how many beans are planted. Sight down the row to see how many came up.

BEEF CATTLE: "Uncertainty will temper beef cattle prices in the coming year." I read this phrase in an economic report last year and recognized it as one of the most profound predictions of all time.

Watch out for the cattle cycle! Those familiar with livestock markets will remember the cattle cycle is not a large machine with pedals.

The cattle cycle is an economic predictor that says cattle numbers will peak and decline on approximately a 16-year cycle. Even though this hasn't happened in the past 50 years, the cattle cycle remains a good way to start a conversation.

HOGS: Hog markets will remain variable in the coming months. Producers should be able to root out a profit, however. (Sorry, I couldn't resist that.)

Much depends upon the price of feed and the price of hogs. Watch the hog-corn ratio. If this ratio gets out of whack sell whatever you have and hunker down until things get better.

MILK: Dairy cows will suffer a let-down during the first few months of the year. Watch Minnesota-Wisconsin cheese prices for trends in fluid markets. If the government offers to buy cows, sell them. If you sold cows in the last buyout, buy some more — and sell them again!

ZEBRAS: Economists have learned zebras are an indicator species for the exotic animal market. When the price of zebras is up, camels, kangaroos, wallabies, etc. are likewise.

The big exception is hippos. When hippos go down everything else goes up. Avoid taking a bath with hippos.

Sell zebras and hippos whenever you can. Buy hogs with the proceeds. Hogs taste better.

Have a good year.

Pond's Magic Plant Food

I've been reading about gardens again. After years of gardening inactivity, I've revived the old rituals once more.

Everyone knows garden fever begins with reading and ends with digging in the dirt. The avid gardener reads seed catalogs, gardening magazines — even fertilizer bags — in the never-ending quest for knowledge.

Then, the garden enthusiast plows his patch. That's what I do, anyway. It's my policy to plow the garden at the same time every year: When it's too dry in the fall, too wet in the spring, and too late to change my mind.

Next, I buy some seeds. This is the exciting part of gardening for me, buying seeds. Hope springs eternal in the hearts and minds of those who purchase seeds.

"I'll have six pounds of potatoes, half-a-pound of corn, and a pound of peas," I tell the clerk (as if I have some idea how much I'll need). If growing vegetables was half as easy as buying seeds, we would have the freezer full in no time.

There's something about leaving a store with all those seeds that gives a person a jolt of optimism. Gophers, and chickens, and gigantic weeds would probably laugh at my armload of seeds.

I had to chuckle recently when I saw a rack of seeds in the grocery. Grocery store racks are famous for those little packages containing 2 "g" of seed. I don't know what "g" stands for, but it isn't gallons, I can tell you that.

Last week I saw a package of sweet corn seed containing 20 grams. The package cost $1.20. Twenty grams is .044 lb., and according to my calculations this sweet corn seed costs something over $27 per pound.

I stood around for a long time, hoping someone would buy one of these packages. If someone buys one, a little man in a clown suit jumps out from behind the rack shouting, "April fool! Ha, Ha, Ha! We got you again."

I noticed a similar product in my own home recently. My wife has a favorite fertilizer she uses for house plants. It comes in a twelve-ounce bottle with a little eye-dropper in the top. Twelve ounces costs $3.69.

The label on this little bottle says "Liquid Plant Food 10-15-10." Farmers in the crowd will recognize this as 10% nitrogen, 15% phosphorus, and 10% potassium. Directions on the bottle call for seven drops of this magic elixir per quart of water, to be used each time you water the plants.

Last week I bought a 50 lb. bag of 16-16-16 fertilizer for $8.50 (which I thought was outrageous). I think I can make the house plant fertilizer for around 15 cents a bottle, not counting the eye-dropper.

Then, I can buy a horse and a big, ol' wagon, and hit the road selling Pond's Magic Plant Food for $3.50 a bottle. When I get rich, I'll buy a new tractor and plow my garden at the right time for a change.

Save Money — Shower Outdoors

Saving money has become a popular subject. Newspapers are filled with new and amazing ideas for saving our dough.

I read recently about a guy in Miami who made a million dollars just by saving and scrimping on his meager salary. He packs his lunch every day; and his wife works at home, supplementing her pathetic wardrobe by shopping at garage sales and second-hand stores.

In 1993 this man's wife bought only a pair of shorts and some tennis shoes! This year she hopes to get a blouse.

That kind of story doesn't bother me, though. I figure anybody who can find a wife who will live like that deserves whatever he gets.

The stories that get me are the ones that suggest people should fool themselves into saving money. Schemes like, "Toss your pocket change into a secure container when you come home each evening. A container that has to be broken or pried open will keep you from dipping back into it."

This missive explains that 50 cents a day adds up to $182 a year. If the whole family does this, all of your cash will be in the jar within a few weeks. Starvation is only a matter of time after that.

A better plan, in my opinion, is to take your paycheck to the bank each month and have it converted into coins. Then, put the coins in a safe deposit box until you want to buy something.

You will soon find that buying things is more work than it's worth; so most of the money stays in the safe deposit until the end of the year. Then, you can take your cash out and send it to the guy with the million dollars so he can buy his wife some clothes.

My favorite money saving idea is the water-saving shower. This concept takes two forms: A family can save water (and money) by shortening the amount of time spent in the shower, or they can save by inserting a gismo in the shower head to stop the water from coming out.

Most folks go for the gismo and call this a "water-saver" shower. No one stops to consider that less water coming out of the shower causes a person to stay longer.

I stayed at a motel in Colorado last fall where the water-saver showers were quite proficient. As I was leaving, a man told the clerk at the desk, "My room was fine — and everyone here has been very nice, but that shower is the most ridiculous thing I've ever seen."

This place had folks staying an extra day just to finish their shower.

Even more dangerous than water-saving showers is the new toilet paper cropping up in service stations these days. Someone has decided they can save money by making toilet paper rolls larger, but narrower. So restrooms are stocking huge rolls of toilet paper five miles long and two-inches wide!

I would sure like to meet the guy who dreamed up that scam. If it happens to be that guy with a million dollars and the naked wife, I hope she drowns him in his water-saving shower.

It's Time For A Round Tax

It's that time of year again: That glorious time of year when the IRS tells us how much to send, and the politicians invent new ways to spend.

There's been a lot of talk around Congress about revamping the tax system and replacing it with a flat tax. This would allow everyone to pay a set percentage of their income; and we wouldn't have to juggle such a pile of paperwork, trying to figure out how much we owe.

That sounds fine to me, but I've always favored a "round tax" over a flat one. A round tax is similar to a flat tax, in that everyone pays the same percentage. The big difference is we wouldn't have to pay a round tax at a certain time each year; we'd just pay it when we got around to it.

I was surprised this week to learn that some folks actually look forward to tax time. That's because they expect to get a refund.

By paying more than they owe each month, some taxpayers use withholding taxes as a forced savings — and count on their yearly refund for paying bills, or funding vacations.

It's a good way to save if you don't have good control of yourself throughout the year.

I applied the same principle years ago when I was feeding pigs. Each spring, I would buy a few pigs and some feed. Then I'd just keep buying feed, and buying feed, and buying feed until the pigs got big enough to eat.

When I sold the pigs, I always got my feed money back, along with most of the cash I paid for the pigs. In the good years, I'd have enough left over to buy some fish bait.

That experience taught me that raising pigs is a real good way to tie up your money so you can't spend it. Sending your dough to Washington, D.C., should have the same effect.

A little boy in Iowa learned the same thing when he began pestering his mother for a hundred dollars. The little guy's mother ignored him as long as she could, but he kept asking and asking until she finally said, "Look, John, if you want $100 so bad, why don't you pray to God for it?"

So, he did. Day after day John prayed for $100. When nothing happened after a couple of weeks, he decided he'd better send God a letter and see what was holding up the money.

The postal service saw the letter was addressed to God, and just naturally believed it must be for the President; so they sent it on to the White House. The President's staff opened the letter, and thought it was so cute they took up a collection to send the kid $30 (thinking this would seem like a lot of money to a little boy).

John was so happy when he got the $30, he sat down immediately and wrote a "thank you" note to God.

"Dear God," he wrote, "Thanks for the money. Too bad you had to send it through Washington, D.C.. They took out 70% as usual."

Guess Again, And Go Sit Down

One advantage of being a writer is you get to comment on nearly everything. Even if you don't know what you're talking about, you still get to comment.

The main disadvantage is that someone might take you seriously. Writers can be crazier than Rush Limbaugh, and some folks still take them seriously. It's amazing.

I was reminded of this when I read about new techniques for teaching spelling to elementary students. Even though I may not know what I'm talking about, I just can't resist commenting.

Readers may have heard about the modern approach to spelling instruction, called "Guess and Go." This system teaches kids to spell words any way they want — but just keep on writing. This is contrived to encourage a child's creativity and reduce his or her inhibitions about writing.

Theory says children will write more frequently and more fluently if they don't have to worry about details, like spelling and grammar. Then, after these youngsters are so fluent they just can't control themselves, we can teach them how to spell.

This logic has some flaws, I think.

First this thesis assumes writing is generally good — and children are inhibited. There are two misses, right off the bat.

Everyone knows writing can be very bad; and whatever we can do to inhibit children is probably a good idea.

Second, the "Guess and Go" theory suggests there is plenty of time to learn spelling and grammar after everyone has become rich and famous.

On the contrary, high school teachers will tell us their students aren't nearly as rich and famous as some of them think they are; and many will still be guessing and going when they are fifty years old.

You can see I'm from the old school when it comes to spelling. Even though mistakes creep into this column occasionally, there's no way to prove the typesetter didn't make them.

When I went to school "guess and go" meant "guess again, and go sit down." We had entire days devoted to spelling exercises.

On those days our teacher would construct the nastiest list of spelling words she could put together, and then line everyone up and embarrass us as much as possible.

Those were the days when people thought inhibitions were good for children. My school taught inhibitions right along with the regular subjects.

For me this reveals the major fallacy in modern theories for teaching writing. Today's educators seem to think writers are a creative and magnanimous lot who want to contribute great ideas to society.

The old teachers knew better. The old teachers knew the greatest inspiration for writers is not the urge to create.

I think writers of my generation would agree, the real motivation for most of us is revenge.

Looking For A Corner

There's a lot of history in the old farm buildings around the country. The style and architecture of these buildings tells us something about the heritage of the original owners and the type of agriculture they were accustomed to.

Farm buildings contain a number of clues as to what sort of person designed them. The shed with small doors and six-foot ceilings was built by a guy who stood five-foot-four and never expected his kids to be any taller.

The big barn with a huge haymow was constructed when the milk price was good and there were six kids to help with the chores. The little tin shed went up after the fluid market went sour, and the farmer decided a few hogs could help pay the light bill.

The first buildings on most farms were the house and the barn. Others were added when prices were good, or after the farm made enough money to expand facilities. When a new barn was built the old one became a calfbarn or a shop and garage.

A new structure was generally built in the most useful

location, but many farmers have wished they could rearrange buildings that were already in place. The old saying, "Tear it all down and start over," was coined by the second generation of farm families.

When I was a kid we rented a farm that had a round barn. This old barn was made of brick and had a silo in the middle. The silo was surrounded by a manger for feeding livestock.

The circular arrangement made sense in the days of chopped-hay and pitchforks. Because cattle are smaller at the front than at the rear, a larger number can eat from a round bunk at any given time.

But modern technology changed the way people feed cattle, and the old barn fell into disrepute as a machinery storage. If you've ever backed machinery into a round barn with a silo in the middle, you will appreciate what a mess that is.

A person with this kind of storage has to plan his farming carefully. He is forever pulling out the baler to get to the mowing machine.

No-till farming was invented by a man who owned a round barn — just because he never could get to his plow!

Stacking hay in a barn like this isn't any picnic, either. No matter how carefully you stack the bales, there are holes and cracks big enough to drop a dog through. It's no place for a perfectionist, I can tell you that.

Sometimes I wonder about the old round barn where we used to farm. It was still standing and in good repair the last time I drove by.

My dad used to joke that old barn was fine for storage, but a man couldn't work there for any length of time. If a fellow had to go to bathroom, he could spend all day looking for a corner.

There He Goes! Shoot! Shoot!

The anti-hunting fraternity suffered a setback when the U.S. Supreme Court turned down a constitutional challenge to a Montana law that prohibits interfering with hunters. The Montana law states, "No person may disturb an individual engaged in the lawful taking of an animal with the intent to dissuade the individual or otherwise prevent taking of the animal."

The court challenge was made on behalf of a man who was protesting a bison hunt several years ago. This fellow stood between hunters and bison and shouted, "Don't shoot!"

Many states have adopted hunter harassment laws in recent years, but they are completely uncalled-for in my opinion. Why don't we just pass a law stating, "It shall be unlawful to do anything totally stupid within this state."

Then, when a guy jumps out of the bushes yelling, "Don't shoot!" the authorities can just load him up and take him to jail.

The Montana law is riddled with loopholes by comparison. How can you keep people from disturbing a hunter?

I've disturbed plenty of hunters over the years. The main difference between me and the guy in Montana is he shouts, "Don't shoot!" whereas I yell, "There he goes! Shoot! Shoot! Shoot!"

The effect is the same. I've saved more critters than all the protesters put together.

Most folks don't realize the woods is full of anti-hunters during big game seasons. The really smart ones dress like hunters and drive an old pickup truck — with one or two spark plug wires removed.

Then they putt-putt down the road looking for hunters. When a hunter steps out of the woods, the anti-hunter is on him like mustard on your best shirt.

The anti-hunter putts up in his old pickup and shouts, "How ya doin'? Seen anything yet?" If you try to get away, he shouts louder. If you run, he laughs.

Some turn off their engine and pretend to speak quietly. Then, the truck roars and backfires when they start it up again. These guys would drive an old John Deere if it didn't look so obvious.

I don't know about you, but I've never seen a game animal within two hours of bumping into the folks with the trucks. I'll hide in the woods rather than face them on the roadside.

Anti-hunters are even worse on a waterfowl hunt. They wear an orange hat and pretend to be a friend of yours.

If you let them into the blind, these fellows keep bobbing their heads to see if those specks are really geese or some type of small aircraft. If they have a duck call, they blow on it. If they have a dog, they bring him along.

States like Montana might as well recognize the split between hunters and anti-hunters is not as clean as it seems. Those guys jumping out of the bushes yelling "Don't shoot!" are harmless compared to the folks we take right along with us.

I've never hunted in Montana, and now I can see why. The first time I yelled, "There he goes! Shoot! Shoot!" some eager deputy would probably nab me and throw me in jail.

The Family Tree

I have never been much on genealogies. I figure my known relatives are scary enough. There's no need to go looking for skeletons.

My father was the same way. He never wanted to trace his ancestors. "What if we find a bunch of horse thieves and carpetbaggers?" he said.

That's what I was thinking when a woman called from South Dakota this week; and when a lady phoned from Oregon a few weeks before. Both were Ponds. One traces her family to Iowa, the other to Colorado.

The woman from South Dakota said, "You'll probably think I'm crazy for calling someone I don't know. But your stories remind me so much of my father and uncles, I just had to call."

She has researched the Pond family tree, and I appreciated her call — even though the reference to being "crazy" frightened me a little. I told her my family wasn't big on genealogies. We never had time for a family tree. The closest we've gotten is the family history my mother put together years ago.

Mother's history doesn't fool around, either. She takes our branch of the family and tells who was descended from whom. None of this wild editorializing one finds in some genealogies. Her history is short and practical. There are so many in the last three generations, we needed a book just to keep track of the kids.

My South Dakota caller has gone quite a bit further. She says the Ponds left England in 1630 — with their neighbors the Winthrops. They landed in Massachusetts.

There were three brothers. She has good records on two of them, but the third seems to have gotten lost.

"That's my branch," I thought. We're always getting lost. If it weren't for the other two brothers, we probably would have landed in the West Indies.

Nobody knows why the Ponds left England, or whether they planned to land in Massachusetts. (That's their business, as far as I'm concerned.)

"What's your dad's name?" the South Dakota woman asked.

"My dad is Paul; but we're from Ohio. We don't have any horse thieves in our family," I said quickly.

"Oh, we have a Paul. He was the son of Samuel. Samuel was born in 1835. What's your grandfather's name?" she asked.

"My grandfather was William," I said. "Hey, wait a minute! I'm not that old!"

"William is a popular name in my family," the lady said. "So is Robert. There were a lot of Johns, too." (Anyone who thinks I'm going to fool with that one has a devious mind.)

We had a nice conversation, and I sent the woman a copy of Mother's family history. I don't think she'll get much out of it, though.

I whited-out everyone I thought might be a bit suspicious.

Mother Did It With Gravy

My television reports today's teenagers are worried about their future. A news report says a survey asked high school seniors if they expected their lives to be better than the lives of their parents. Forty-seven percent of these teenagers said, "No."

Authors of the survey claim this shows how bad the economy has become. These researchers say young people should expect to eclipse their parents' standard of living. Each generation should have the ability to spend more money than the last.

That depends upon one's perspective, I guess. Maybe it's a good sign if teenagers don't expect to have more things than their parents. They might spend more time with their children and get off the merry-go-round society has built for itself.

My generation has more money than our parents ever thought about, but I don't think we're any happier. Nobody wants to return to the "good old days," but there's something to be said for learning to do without — just in case we ever have to.

All of this came to mind when my wife and I went out

for dinner recently. We don't go out each month like the marriage counselors suggest a couple should. We skip a lot of months between dinners out. When we do go, I write about it in my column so I'll have a record that we went.

Dinner at the restaurant reminded me of the meals my mother used to fix. Restaurant meals are nothing like we had at home, but eating out always reminds me that Mother fed our entire family for a month on what two meals cost at the restaurant.

Others of my generation will remember how she did it, too. Mother did it with gravy. She could make gravy out of anything, and once we had the gravy, we almost always had something to put it on.

We put gravy on bread, toast, potatoes, rice, vegetables; and when times were tough, we put gravy on gravy. Can you imagine how many meals a person can make with $40 worth of gravy?

Mother had to have meat to make the gravy, of course, but we always had meat. My third grade teacher explained it this way, "You farm kids never have to worry about food. If you run out of money, you can always go out and kill a pig."

We never killed a pig just to make gravy, but I suppose we could if we wanted to. Mother made gravy from small bits of ham, steak, chicken, rabbit, hamburger — even bologna. Some readers may balk at bologna gravy, but it's good if you're hungry.

Another economical dish my mother used to make is corn starch. Corn starch is made by mixing and heating milk, sugar, and corn starch. It makes a hot, creamy breakfast to be served with toast on the side.

Corn starch might be short on fiber and it certainly wasn't invented by a nutritionist, but it had several things going for it. Corn starch was hot, it tasted good — and best of all, it was made by your mother.

Research has shown that last part is still more important than all of the nutrients money can buy.

Keep Your Mind Open And Your Door Shut

I read an article recently about the need for teaching values in schools. The author says schools have stopped teaching values and need to design a curriculum to deal with these issues.

I find that astonishing. This country may be confused, but old-fashioned values, like taking responsibility for your actions, respecting authority, and working for a living are not that foreign to most classrooms. Teachers can handle that kind of stuff.

The real issue is whether teachers are imparting beliefs parents can agree on; but from what I've heard, many parents aren't doing so hot in the values department themselves. I'm not sure a referendum is a good idea.

Can you imagine the time and controversy involved with outlining a set of beliefs teachers should extol, and a list of virtues they shouldn't have to worry about?

Schools have always taught values in one way or another. My old chemistry teacher is a good example.

Mr. Paulding (not his real name) crammed more values into 45 minutes than any curriculum committee could dream up in a month. He taught some chemistry, too, but old-fashioned virtue was his primary mission.

Mr. Paulding could leap from his Krebs Cycle and tackle the foibles of socialism faster than Superman can button his shirt. Then, we had 40 minutes of lecture — but nobody had to take any notes.

Our chemistry teacher didn't need any values committee, either. All he needed was some prodding from an alert sophomore who was a little behind in his homework.

The man was an excellent teacher, but everyone knew his views were tilted to the right. Even he must have known rounding up welfare recipients and sending them all to Siberia wasn't really in the cards.

In those days, we got our right-wing views in chemistry class and the left flank was guarded by Miss Herstbach. I have often wondered how those teachers of the '50s would adapt to modern systems of integrated learning.

Can you imagine Mr. Paulding and Miss Herstbach team-teaching? The first time our chemistry teacher shared his views on affirmative action, Miss Herstbach would have clobbered him with her music stand.

Those days are gone, I'm afraid, but common sense tells us kids don't just swallow whatever we tell them, anyway. My wife and I tried to teach our kids to keep an open mind and think through the issues, but I'm not sure how successful we were.

When our kids were small, and refused to eat their broccoli or try something new, my wife would say, "Well, maybe you just need to open up your mind a little."

This worked fine, until our son was about nine years old — and his bedroom became a disaster area. My wife walked into the boy's bedroom one day and said, "This room looks like a pig sty! I don't see how anyone could stand to live in a mess like this."

Russell thought about that for a second, and said, "Well, maybe you just need to open up your mind a little."

The Hunting Diary

I always enjoy those "Year In Review" pieces we read in the newspapers. You know, those early January missives that report, "The city fixed the sewer lines in March. Morgan's Lake south of town dried up in May."

I'm not sure I've ever done one of those pieces, but I've read enough stories from the past to know they aren't terribly accurate.

The problem with old stories is there's no way to separate what really happened from the writer's view of those events. The "Year in Review" pieces always remind me of my son's hunting diary.

My son, Russell, began his hunting and fishing diary when he was about 12, and it quickly evolved into a classic case of creative writing. I attended nearly all of the trips described in my son's diary, but my version of these events was lost in the editing.

October 21, 1988 is a good example. That was the day I killed the biggest deer I have ever been associated with; but Russell's diary barely mentions the event.

Other entries for the day include: "I hunted quail down by the bull pen. Got four birds with seven shots; one high, crossing shot through the trees, two straight-aways, and a nice shot on a bird that jumped behind me.

"Weather was overcast, with a breeze from the east. Wind caused most of my misses. The dog jumped two pheasants out of range.

"My shotgun has too much drop at the heel, causing me to shoot low. Need a new gun, better dog, bigger game bag."

Then, in the last sentence of the day, the diary states blandly, "Dad shot a deer."

No mention of a "huge buck," "nice deer," or even "Dad was better than average today." If I had fallen off a cliff, landed in the creek, and killed four ducks with my impact, the diary would have said, "Dad was extra clumsy while hunting near the creek."

May 4, 1989 wasn't much better. This entry says, "Went bass fishing and camping with Dad, Mark, and Dan. Water was muddy, fishing slow the first day. Much better the second day.

"I caught a four-pound bass and two three-pounders. Mark and Dan did okay, too. They caught some nice crappies from the dock.

"I caught the most fish on a jig with a chartreuse grub on it. Mark used a black, plastic worm with a yellow tail."

"Dad uses worms and never weighs his fish."

How To Eat Confetti

Every town needs a festival. Whether it's Pickle Days, The Harvest Fest, or Spring Fling, there's nothing like a community celebration to promote business and bring people together.

The little town where I grew up has a celebration called the "Fall Festival." Folks say it started with the pioneers who first settled the area. Once the harvest was over the settlers would throw a big party, squeeze a bunch of apples, and get sick together.

The event was so successful the city council wanted to have a spring celebration, too, but nobody could come up with a good name for a spring festival. The council asked farmers to suggest names based upon activities on the farm.

"Just think about what you do on the farm in spring," they suggested.

"We clean out the barn in the spring," one farmer said. "If you want to sponsor a festival called 'Dung-out Days' it's okay with me, but I'm not coming."

Soon after that the Fall Festival fell into controversy.

The Lions Club had the confetti concession for many years, and the Festival Committee wanted to outlaw confetti as too dangerous.

Several people testified they ate confetti with their hot-dogs every year, and a few reported round flakes of paper stuck in their ears. One gentleman said he ate more confetti than candy apples, and considered it better for him from a dietary standpoint.

I can't speak for the other kids, but for me, the Fall Festival was never the same after they took the confetti away.

Then, once the confetti was gone, people began objecting to the gambling. You can't blame these folks for griping. They had lost a lot of money.

There were some strange games of chance in those days. The one I remember most involved a mouse on a horizontal roulette wheel.

The wheel was surrounded by pint jars that were painted black and given a number. When a mouse was placed on the spinning wheel, the jar he ran into determined the winning number — like a high-speed game of musical chairs. A second mouse was kept in reserve in case this one got dizzy before the night was over.

The Fall Festival had other games of chance, but the biggest gamble a person could take was getting on the carnival rides. Everyone knew the rides were risky, and the people running them were even more dangerous than the machinery.

The festival committee changed its name to "Harvest Days" a few years ago, but I suspect the kids have as much fun as they ever did.

This event will never be the same for me, though. There's something about getting hit with a handful of confetti that will never be matched by modern entertainment.

Nothing To Sniff At

The use of animals for drug detection has finally gone too far. Everybody got along fine with dope-sniffing dogs, but police departments are having problems with the more exotic drug-sniffers.

This week I read that the Freeport, Illinois police fired their drug-sniffing pig, Louis Lee. The pot-bellied pig was cited for sloppy personal hygiene, lack of altitude, and poor work habits.

The Chief of Police accused Louis Lee of messing up a squad car and refusing to wake up when he was called. "The pig dumped in the squad car . . . You had to hold him up to smell a bookshelf. One time we called him when he was sleeping, and he refused to get up," the chief said.

A Chicago Tribune story says several U.S. cities and some European jurisdictions employ pot-bellied pigs for drug detection. Only Louis Lee has been accorded such shabby treatment, however.

The Freeport police should be ashamed of themselves, in my opinion. This is a pig, for gosh sakes. If the cops want somebody to sniff bookshelves they should get a giraffe.

I knew this would happen when pot-bellied pigs became popular years ago. Everybody thought they needed a pig, but most people expected their pig to act like a dog.

So we had folks building little pig houses for the critters to sleep in. Then they put leashes on their porkers and led 'em up and down the street. Now the cops have decided the pigs' keen sense of smell makes them ideal drug-sniffers.

Well, I've got news for them: A pig is a pig — is a pig! If these folks don't understand pigs, they should get a dog.

Pigs are smarter than most people realize. We just have to see things from the hogs' perspective.

That mess in the squad car is a prime example. Louis Lee wouldn't have done that if they had given him a badge like the other cops have. You can't just take a pig out and throw him in the back of a squad car without a hat, badge or anything. Louis probably thought he was being arrested!

Pigs are clean animals, but you have to treat them with respect. I wouldn't give the pig a gun, but some type of uniform is essential.

The Freeport police fired Louis for being too short to sniff bookshelves. That just shows how little they know about these creatures.

A pig can sniff a bookshelf anytime he wants, but he won't climb up there to do it. Give him some time, and the pig will knock the bookcase over, sniff the literature, and wallow in the romance novels. He just needs some time to think things through.

It's too late for Louis, though. His termination is final, and his owner took him home to play with her kids.

The children are teaching Louis to play a toy piano, and he seems to be getting his confidence back. Everyone is hoping the pig can keep his nose clean long enough to establish a second career.

All Aboard!

Faithful readers may recall a column in which I mentioned our trip to San Francisco. More likely, readers couldn't care less whether I went to San Francisco or not.

You've seen this before. Anyone who takes a vacation is constantly lurking nearby, awaiting a gap in the conversation so they can tell others where they went.

"Oh, yes I love this bean dip. It always reminds me of the luau William and I attended in Hawaii."

In addition to punishing readers who may have pulled this kind of stunt, I mention San Francisco for a more personal reason: I had to begin this story some way.

Besides, I think everyone should visit cities like this. If I have to go, I see no reason others should be able to get out of it.

My wife says we had a wonderful time, and I suppose we did. Everyone should visit the Golden Gate Bridge, Fisherman's Wharf, Cannery Row. I wrote this stuff down as evidence we had been there, and kept my trolley ticket for further proof.

Those who ride San Francisco trolleys will understand

how I kept my ticket. The trolley master is so busy jumping on and off, cramming on passengers, he doesn't have time to pick up the tickets. Our ticket man was so enthused about loading more people the trolley had to stop every few blocks to let folks off who never planned to get on in the first place.

It seems that California has a law against riding in the back of pickups, but the state encourages people to hang on the side of trolley cars.

I have no reason to question the safety of these vehicles, though. They have a bell to warn pedestrians the contraption is coming, and there's a hole in the floor with a stick for a brake. Besides, people are free to jump off any time they want.

Nobody got hurt on our ride, but a couple of folks wandered off kind of gingerly. That's just the normal trampling one would expect with a big load like that.

The trolley ride reminded me of taking hogs to the auction when I was a kid. The main difference is you could never load hogs onto a trolley. They've got more sense than that.

My brothers and I used to walk into the hog barn on auction day and holler, "All aboard — Market Street, Porker Heaven, Sausage Alley. Have your tickets ready!" Then, we'd start pushing and shoving pigs up the ramp until the truck was full.

Once the truck was loaded, we would drive off real slow, so the pigs didn't fall down and get to fighting. The trolley operates the same way — except they never speed up.

We got on at Union Square and sat down beside an old Chinese man. The trolley headed off toward Fisherman's Wharf. The Chinese guy jumped ship several blocks later, but I swear we saw him three more times before we got to the Bay.

Every few minutes I'd tell my wife, "Hey, there's that Chinese guy again. I think he's gaining on us."

I'm glad we went to San Francisco and rode the trolley, though. If I ever go to Hawaii, this will give me something to talk about at the luau.

We Should Have Been Warned

The debate over tort reform and frivolous lawsuits seems so unnecessary and divisive. Some of the country's top legal beagles say most of those outrageous court settlements we've been reading about could have been prevented with a simple warning.

The woman scalded with hot coffee could have been warned about holding coffee cups between her legs; and the man who crashed his bicycle while riding in the dark could have been told he needed a light for riding at night

Bicycle manufacturers might adopt the old Cornish prayer:

From Ghoulies and Ghosties
And long leggity Beasties
And things that go "Bump, Whomp, Splat!" in the night.
Your light must protect you.

I reworded that a little; but a similar caution could have prevented the damage to my Subaru a few years ago. It's a long story, but faithful readers may recall the day my pickup truck crashed into my Subaru — through no fault of my own.

None of this would have happened if General Motors had put a warning label on their trucks. A statement like, "Mr. Pond, you idiot! You can't pull this truck when it doesn't have a driver," might have prevented the whole thing. (They're lucky I didn't sue.)

Some folks think a person who does something stupid doesn't deserve a big court settlement, but that's not the way I look at it. My lawyer friends say they try to get the biggest cash award they can for their dumbest clients. That's because they know we're going to waste most of it.

I think the best way to prevent these calamities and frivolous lawsuits is a nationwide warning system. A federal commission on warnings would go a long way toward predicting the stupid things people might try next.

Just cautioning folks to stay in bed — or stay out of bed in some cases — could prevent a lot of grief.

A contingent of lawmakers in Washington state has adopted that philosophy, and is working to require warnings on marriage licenses. Sponsors of this legislation say folks are making marital decisions with their eyes closed. People should be warned that "Marriage is serious business."

If this proposal passes, marriage licenses in Washington would declare, "Neither you nor your spouse is the property of the other," and "The laws of this state affirm your right to enter into this marriage and at the same time to live within the marriage free from violence and abuse."

Whatever our feelings about matrimony, property rights, and violence, there's something about a warning on a marriage license that leaves me skeptical. I think most of us can remember, if people listened to warnings, there probably wouldn't be any marriages.

Marriage Makes A Person Deaf

There's something about marriage that affects a person's hearing. Getting married doesn't make people deaf, but it certainly affects their hearing.

A good example is a woman I met at a trade show a few months ago. This lady has written and published a book, and we were talking about publishing costs and book markets, when she said, "My husband thinks I should raise the price of my book, but I don't think so. What do you think?"

I launched into a discourse on discounts and marketing costs and ended with my opinion that folks will pay a reasonable price for something they like; but they won't pay two cents for something they didn't want in the first place.

The woman listened attentively and then replied, "Okay, that's what I'll do. I'll raise my price."

As she walked away I thought to myself, "Now why didn't she say that when her husband told her exactly the same thing I did?"

That's what marriage does to folks. It plugs up their ears.

My next example is my wife — in case you hadn't guessed.

Connie is an avid gardener. She doesn't grow vegetables, but she's crazy about roses.

My wife reads all the magazines and garden columnists and tries to follow their suggestions as closely as possible. The problem is many garden writers won't tell you anything about fertilizers.

They might give you an analysis, or even a brand, of fertilizer to use, but they won't say how much. If a writer gave farmers directions like that they'd beat him to death with his clipboard. A fertilizer analysis is worthless if you don't know the application rate.

I'm no flower gardening expert, but I have been around the bean patch a few times. I have studied crops and soils, base saturation, cation exchange capacity, and several other things I don't fully understand.

I've hobnobbed with soil scientists, agronomists, horticulturists, county agents, and guys who sell snake oil over the phone. So, I thought my opinion might have some value.

I told my wife, "Our soil is pretty good for phosphorus and potassium, but the roses will respond to more. On the other hand, I see no reason to apply more phosphorus than nitrogen with the soils we have around here."

I said the garden writers live in a different area. They have different soils, and every one of them is saying something different, anyway.

But, did she hear me? Please refer back to paragraph one.

Then, last night, my wife was reading about a fellow who owns 600 rose bushes. He says rose fertilizers don't have enough nitrogen; so he applies 1/2 cup of 15-10-10 per plant — and gives them more about halfway through the summer.

"I'm glad to see someone agrees with me about the nitrogen," I said, "But that's quite a bit of fertilizer. Depending on his plant spacing, that could be three or four hundred pounds of nitrogen per acre."

My wife looked up from her magazine and said, "Well, I'm sure he knows a lot more about roses than you do."

Give 'Em Another Shot And Call Me In The Morning

We should never underestimate the value of home remedies in agriculture. Amid all of our modern technology, nothing surpasses the home remedy for providing relief in the most difficult situations.

If we study these home-grown nostrums we generally find they provide more humor for the practitioner than benefit to the patient. Any farmer can tell you a sense of humor is about all that can be salvaged from many situations

This was brought home to me recently when a friend called with a question. He said a young friend bought a steer for the purpose of taking it to the county fair next summer, but the youngster later learned the steer was wilder than a March hare.

The animal was so unruly the owners considered giving it tranquilizers until it could be brought under control in its new surroundings. Then someone suggested, "Get the cheapest fifth of whiskey you can find, and administer it as a drench. This should calm the steer down so you can work with it."

My friend's question was this, "What will that do to the steer?"

"I don't know," I told him. "But if it works, the poor critter will be attending meetings before he's a year-and-a-half old."

We talked about some other home remedies and marveled at the frequency with which whiskey or rum is the main ingredient. One wonders whether the medication ever gets to the animals.

The old recipes for milk substitutes are a good example. These concoctions always contain some form of cow's milk or concentrated milk, a little sugar — and a shot of whiskey. (The better ones substitute eggnog for the cow's milk.)

The old sheep ranchers used to tell the vet, "I did just as you said, Doc. I mixed the cow's milk and the sugar, and heated it real slow; then I put in a shot of whiskey."

"And you gave this to the lambs, every four hours?" the vet asks.

"Lambs?!" the shepherd exclaims.

This reminded my friend of a fellow who asked his neighbor to come over and look at his wheat one spring. The wheat was yellow, the stand wasn't very good, and dry weather was taking its toll on the new seeding.

The two men walked around the field for almost an hour. Finally, the neighbor said, "Well, it looks to me like you should do what the fellow down the road does. You should put a pint of whiskey in your hip pocket and wear your sunglasses.

"Then walk your fields from one end to the other. By the time you get back to the house, this wheat won't look bad at all."

Be Sure To Wear Your Mask

The list of things that may be hazardous to our health grows longer every day. Health screening tests conducted at the World Pork Expo several years ago showed that raising hogs can lead to a unique set of health problems.

A news report says 249 pork producers and 155 non-producers were screened for hearing loss, lung function, cholesterol levels, and skin lesions. While differences between hog farmers and non-hog farmers were generally slight, a greater degree of hearing loss was found in swine producers than in non-producers taking the tests.

This leads to speculation that exposure to pig squeals might cause hearing loss. Pig squeals are said to register 105 decibels — about the same as a high school dance. Many folks say that's why hog producers make the best dance chaperons.

The Pork Expo tests also showed hog raisers had the greatest degree of hearing loss in their left ear. Doctors seemed puzzled by this finding, but I'm not. Anyone who cradles baby pigs in his left arm, while clipping needle teeth and notching ears with his right, can tell us which ear gets the damage.

Those who examine the ears of swine producers will find the left earlobe is generally more chewed for the same reason.

A second finding of the Pork Expo screenings was that most pork producers don't wear hearing protection. Some were leery of wearing headsets for jobs such as sorting hogs. A few mentioned the discomfort a person feels from multiple hoof-prints on his back.

On the other hand, studies have shown that wives of swine producers often wear earplugs when sorting livestock with their husbands. The same is true for wives who assist with harvesting wheat, vaccinating sheep, or stacking wood.

A third finding of the pork producer testing was that hog farmers generally have good lungs. This might be inherited from pioneer days — when a fellow who couldn't yell never saw his hogs again.

Only 10.5 percent of swine producers in this study were unable to inhale to a minimum acceptable capacity. On the other hand 12.5 percent of swine producers could not exhale to an acceptable level.

Common sense tells us hog farmers will avoid exhaling at all costs. The only folks who can hold their breath longer than a hog farmer are the guys harvesting pearls in the South Pacific.

When I was a kid I could enter the hog barn and do a half hour's worth of chores without exhaling. Then, I would go outside and breathe for a while before finishing the feeding.

The Pork Expo screenings indicated few pork producers wear a mask when working. Doctors believe masks would help prevent respiratory problems.

Hog producers said they aren't opposed to masks. Many claimed the fellow who buys their hogs wears a mask, but that's because of the price he pays for the pigs.

A Sad Christmas Story

Our environmental consciousness has caused value conflicts for Americans. How can we justify cutting a beautiful evergreen to decorate for the short Christmas season? Then, what can one do with a dead tree so it won't wind up buried in a landfill?

This may be a problem in urban areas, but I think it could be avoided with a little planning. Experts say there are three basic remedies for the tree disposal problem:

1. *Buy a live tree and plant it outside after Christmas.*
2. *Get a fake tree.*
3. *Buy a commercial tree and keep some beavers in the garage.*

Purchasing a live tree and replanting it in the back yard has the most appeal for many. Some of these trees will live for years; and when the yard fills up, one can always move — or resort to option #3.

Experts say a few simple precautions can give your living Christmas tree a better chance for survival. First, it's best not to keep a live tree in the house too long.

Many folks like to bring their living tree into the house for a short visit and take it back outside before it gets warm. If we do this over a period of days the tree becomes acclimated to its new home and will soon be going to the door when it wants out.

This can be carried too far, however. Those who want to use the same tree from one Christmas to the next should be aware there is nothing worse than a tree that comes to the door when it wants in!

Option #2 is a hard sell for me. Advocates for manufactured trees claim these creations look so natural you should keep the dog outside for a few days until he gets used to the thing. I can tell the difference, however.

You might have guessed option #3 is my preference. I like a real tree and don't mind supporting the Christmas tree industry. I'll even go out into the national forest and cut my own when I can.

Besides, there are plenty of things one can do with a dead tree. Those who are concerned about appearances might pretend their tree is alive and plant it in the yard soon after Christmas. This satisfies the neighbors that you bought a living tree, and looks perfectly normal when the tree blows down in the first windstorm.

Then, lest we feel bad about being caught with a dead tree, everyone should remember the "Sad Christmas Story." This tale is about a small forest planted by a farmer for choose-and-cut Christmas trees.

Among the farmer's grove of trees was one scraggly, little fir with a bent trunk and a bad case of needle rust. Still, this little tree was hoping it would be the first one chosen when families came to select their Christmas trees.

A few weeks before the big holiday families began arriving at the farm. One by one trees were chosen and taken home for Christmas, until finally, the little fir was the only one left! The little tree was near tears with the prospect that he might not be chosen for a Christmas tree.

Then, just as this poor, little sapling was about to give up hope of ever amounting to anything, along came a big flock of woodpeckers and wiped him out!

The moral of the story? "Being cut for Christmas is not the worst thing that can happen to a tree."

Don't Let Your Body Get You Down

I can't speak for others, but I'm certainly not looking forward to retirement. I see those retired people running up and down the street, riding their exercise bikes, and square dancing four nights a week, and say to myself, "Hey, wait a minute! I thought retirement was supposed to be relaxing!"

I was talking with my brother recently when the conversation turned toward retirement. "I don't worry much about that," I told him. "I'm doing what I want to do, and there's no reason I can't keep doing it as long as my mind holds out."

"Yeah, I see what you mean," he said. "Even if your mind gets a little feeble, it probably won't hurt your writing. It might even help."

Now what do you suppose he meant by that?!

Growing older can be tough, though. The little aches and pains of aging would be more tolerable if a person's mind and body matured in a level progression.

Even at my age, I have days when my mind shouts, "Let's run outdoors and get some work done," but my body says, "Why don't we just lie down here until we get our senses back."

One can imagine what it's like for people who are 85 or 90 years old. These folks have to be careful their minds and bodies don't get to bickering back and forth.

A good example is the 90-year-old golfer who made a hole-in-one in Toronto several years ago. The old fellow tees up on a 140-yard par 3; and with a swing reminiscent of a 20 year-old, he strokes the ball directly into the hole.

We might think this is great for an old-timer to experience the excitement of a hole-in-one, but this fellow's eyes aren't what they used to be. So he never saw his ball go into the cup.

He's good enough to make a hole-in-one, but he can't see where the ball goes!

His playing partner was a young whipper-snapper of about 80, and he saw the ball go down. The partner begins shouting, "Max, you made a hole-in-one! Max, you made a hole-in-one!"

As luck would have it, Max's hearing is on the blink, too; and his hearing-aid was turned down. So he couldn't hear his partner shouting.

Finally, he turns up his hearing-aid; and the partner yells, "It went in, Max. It's a hole-in-one!"

Max says, "No, it couldn't be." Both golfers walk up to the green, and there's the ball — right in the bottom of the cup.

Consider this for a moment. Here we have a 90-year-old man who hits a golf ball well enough to make a hole-in-one; but his eyes won't let him see it, his ears can't hear the cheering, and his mind won't let him believe it.

I don't mean to sound bitter or anything like that, but I've played golf more than 30 years and never made a hole-in-one. When I get to the point where I can't see it, hear it, or believe it, I think I'll just go fishing.

Dance With The One That Brung You

U.S. agriculture has made great progress during the past century. I haven't been around long enough to see the whole thing, but there has been considerable change in the 30-some years since I reached the age of reason.

Today I read corn yields in Indiana averaged 144 bushels per acre last year, while Ohio farmers averaged 139 bushels per acre. This is just a few bushels off the record yields of 1992.

We never saw 100 bushels per acre when I was a kid. Very few people did.

I remember harvesting corn plots near Dayton, Ohio in the early 1960s. The farmer applied 1,000 pounds of 10-10-10 fertilizer per acre — an outrageous amount in those days, and he got 110 bushels per acre.

When I left college a few years later, young farmers throughout the Midwest were organizing corn clubs. Anyone who joined the corn club and produced 100 bushels per acre got his name on a plaque — and the chance to tell everyone about it. If one of those guys got less than 100 bushels today, he would probably go back and rip his name off the plaque.

I credit advances in agriculture to the partnership between farmers and their commercial suppliers, along with universities and U.S.D.A. agencies that have traditionally worked with both.

It's hard for me to imagine agriculture without this long-standing partnership between farmers and government agencies as well as commercial companies. Current thinking and agency ineptitude raise that possibility, however.

Some years ago I talked with a respected farm leader who recounted a conversation he had with the Director of Extension in his state. The two men were discussing the need for universities and cooperative extension to work with farmers. (I'll call the farm leader "Frank" in respect for his privacy.)

Frank had a long and distinguished career with Cooperative Extension before becoming a full-time farmer, but it soon became evident the two men did not agree.

One thing led to another until the extension director said, "The man who lives in the city with four tomato plants has just as much right to help from extension as the commercial farmer. The farmer can get advice from his equipment dealers and the suppliers he buys from. He's not dependent upon the university or his county extension agent for information."

This irritated Frank considerably. "Well, maybe the guy who lives in the city with his tomato plants could get his advice from the store where he bought them. Then we wouldn't need you at all," he shot back.

Those are harsh words, but these are harsh times. Cooperative Extension has had 30 years to figure out what Frank said in two short sentences. In many areas, I'm afraid it's already too late.

Humor Was A Way Of Life

A recent conversation with a bookstore owner reminded me that some folks don't think the way I do. It's a good thing, I suppose, but it's quite a shock to learn I've been swimming out of the current most of the time.

The store owner and I were talking about various types of books (humor, travel, cookbooks, etc.) when the book man said, "Humor doesn't appeal to everyone, but cookbooks do." I agreed with him verbally, but my mind was churning.

Humor doesn't appeal to everyone?! How can that be? Where I grew up humor was a way of life.

I grew up in a farming community, and you won't find many farmers who don't have a keen sense of humor. They have to.

Many of the things that happen on a farm are so totally unpredictable, the only thing folks can do about them is laugh — or cry. It just doesn't seem right for a grown man to spend most of his life crying, so farmers try to find some humor in everything they can.

I remember going to school when I was a kid and seeking out the funniest kids to sit next to. The worst thing that could happen to a farm kid was to get stuck next to some bug-eyed chemistry fiend, or a sour-faced Shakespeare fan. We did everything we could to prevent such a disaster.

Even the teachers had a sense of humor in those days. They had no choice: Losing your sense of humor was a short hop from a nervous breakdown for a small town school teacher.

There were exceptions, though. The one I remember best was Miss Barker (not her real name).

Miss Barker began teaching in the days when schools wouldn't hire a woman teacher if she was married. Then, when she got married, she had to quit teaching.

Most of these young teachers didn't last very long. They found a nice, bachelor farmer, got married, and had to quit teaching.

But the school board knew they had a deal with Miss Barker. Everybody could see she was in this thing for the long haul.

The thing I remember most about Miss Barker was her penchant for denying the humor around her. We did our best to cheer her up, but it never seemed to help.

One of the students would pull something we thought especially amusing, and she would say, "You may have thought that was funny, but I certainly didn't."

"Don't worry Miss Barker," we'd tell her. "You just hang in there, and you'll probably catch-on right away next time."

I often think of Miss Barker when I'm browsing around a bookstore and notice their skimpy, little humor section. I know it's kind of silly, but I can't help looking over my shoulder — expecting to hear Miss Barker saying, "Humor doesn't appeal to everyone. Maybe you'd like one of these nice cookbooks over here under the cat."

Protesters Have All The Fun

There is growing sentiment that the environmental movement is getting out of hand. Much of what started as a good cause has eroded into a media event, staged by those who shun useful labor and would like to eliminate it entirely.

The most entertaining (and destructive) of these events are the protests staged to prevent logging. These are classic social confrontations: The hard-hat, lunch-bucket, venison-eating woodsman against the . . , well, never mind. You already know how I feel.

But the loggers always lose these events. They come out looking bad because they don't know how to deal with a person who chains himself to a tree and then poses for photos.

Most of all the loggers lose because they can't handle the media. Loggers can't handle the media because they don't have good names.

Loggers have names like Frank Jones or Jim Schultz. Demonstrators, on the other hand, have fun names like Doug Fir, Red Woods, or Forest Duff.

A good example is the lady who appeared in a grass

skirt during an anti-logging demonstration near Portland, Oregon. While other demonstrators chained themselves to a gate and dared loggers to open it, this lady wore a skirt made of cedar bark and gave her name as "Cedar Tree."

A bad example, on the other hand, is an altercation in northern Washington, where demonstrators climbed onto the U.S. Forest Service office and jumped up-and-down on the roof until police were able to net them.

These demonstrators had little imagination and refused to give names. They needed a guy with a name like "Lucien Shingles" to make that story more fun.

But what do the loggers and the Forest Service people do when a reporter asks their names? They give them real names or refuse to talk, ruining a potentially good news story.

Imagine what might have happened if the loggers opening the gate in the first example had their names ready. We could have, "Logging was briefly held up when protesters, Red Woods and Olive Branch, chained themselves to a gate and dared loggers to open it.

"Demonstrators reported minor injuries when the gate was pushed open by loggers, Roland Bouncem, Scuffum Badly, and Willy Barker. Bouncem said the gate is heavier some days than others."

Now, we have some news! There's no reason working people can't have fun names, too.

Forest rangers could be Smokey Rabbit or Count DeCampers. A forest administrator might be Carrie Lunch, Paper Shuffles, or Buster Files.

The next time we have one of these forest sit-ins, I want to see some good names on both sides. Why should the protesters have all the fun?

Critters Explained

Everyone who owns animals has a reason. Our motives may not make sense, but being able to explain one's actions is a requirement for personal sanity.

Small-time livestock raisers often have several reasons for keeping animals. Sometimes we just like having a few critters around.

Some of my excuses for keeping animals remind me of the rodeo announcer who was making a valiant attempt to explain the origins of the wild-cow-milking event. The announcer makes this activity sound like a part of everyday life on a ranch.

"The next event, folks, is a true test of a cowboy's ability to perform a chore commonly encountered on the range. There are many instances where a cow loses her calf or fails to claim it, and the cowboy must catch her and milk her out to obtain colostrum milk for the newborn calf.

"In these situations," he explains, "the cowboy may be called upon to rope that cow — and milk her without the aid of a corral or stanchion."

Then, as the announcer is finishing his spiel, a fleet-footed cow bolts from a pen at one end of the arena; and a cowboy on horseback takes up the chase. At one side of the arena waits the designated "mugger," a second cowboy, cracking his knuckles and impatiently gripping a pop bottle in which he hopes to collect a few drops of milk.

The crowd cheers as this entourage circles the arena, and the mounted cowboy finally loops his rope around old bossy's noggin. Now, the mugger dashes forth and tries to throttle the romping and bawling cow while his partner sheds his horse and grabs for the nearest faucet.

Now I ask you, is that a good way to milk a cow? Or an everyday event on the ranch? But the rodeo announcer makes it seem perfectly reasonable!

I look at raising animals the same way: It may not be rational, but if a person can explain why he does it, it's okay with me.

A friend who has a horse, two goats, and a llama tells of an incident which forced him to admit the obvious: Like many other denizens of the backyard, his animals are just pets and weed eaters.

My friend was closing his mail box one day when an eighteen-wheeler with Tennessee plates came rolling down the road from the fruit warehouse. Suddenly the driver slammed on his brakes, bringing the truck to a halt; and began backing up the road.

When the truck was even with Bob's mailbox, the driver said, "Hey, what's that?"

Knowing his llama, Freddy, was in the pasture behind him, Bob was not surprised by the question. "That's a llama," he replied.

"What's it good for?" the trucker inquired.

"Nothing!" Bob laughed.

"Okay. Thanks," the trucker said as he revved his engine and drove on down the road.

Confounded Engineers

I could see this was going to be a doozy. The man at the counter grimaced when I told him where I was going, and the one on the stool got a funny little grin on his face.

It's not that I'm afraid of being lost. I've been lost in some of the nicest places in the world. I subscribe to the old backpackers' philosophy: "If you don't care where you are, you aren't lost."

This was different, though. These guys were having way too much fun giving me directions.

The fellow at the counter took out a huge sheet of paper and began to draw. "To get to Mike Jones' place, you go through town on this road here," he said. "Then you'll see a paved road going off like this, but don't take that.

"You'll go through a little draw here, and the road makes a bend about there. Take the gravel road straight ahead."

He retraced the route and remembered another road off to the left. I should stay away from that one. It would be easy to tell because the gravel was much better than the one I wanted.

He began to frown again; and I could see he was lost, too. His drawing was half way down the paper and only three miles from town. The Jones place was 15 miles out!

The main road continued to the edge of the paper and took a sharp bend to the right. He went back and put in some curves and a few forks. Then he erased a creek and a mountain.

"Now, when you get to the top after coming out of the draw, stay to the right and you'll see some wheat fields and a road — and then another one. Mike's place is on the second road. It's called Jones road." (Naturally.)

I thanked the man for the directions and headed out of town. Then I stopped to look at this homemade map a little closer.

About six miles from town the scale disappeared. One road ran down to the edge and fell off the paper.

I began to wonder if a draw is about the size of a slough, or much larger — like a canyon? Does a good gravel road have big gravel or little gravel?

I went through a draw and turned right at the top. I went a few miles and took a gravel road to the left. It wasn't good gravel though. I'd call it about average.

So I turned around, and finally after many uninhabited miles, I came to a paved road. Now, I was really lost. Other people may drive on paved roads, but I never see pavement when I'm looking for a wheat farmer.

After several wrong turns and a lot of driving, I learned I was on Jones Road early in the expedition, except the county engineer had changed to road name to 10 SW. (So folks wouldn't get lost, I suppose.)

Everyone thinks Lewis and Clark were great explorers, but let's remember, those guys had one big advantage: There weren't any county engineers, running around changing the road names.

Say "Hi" To Susan

Maybe it was the western jacket — or the cowboy boots. The short haircut may have given me away. Whatever it was, they could see me coming.

I was in Oakland, California, and everyone knew I wouldn't be there if I had any kind of choice. The street people must have thought I fell off a turnip truck.

Everybody wanted a dollar for something. One guy needed to buy milk for his cat, and another had just been released from the hospital. He needed bus fare to get home.

These folks dreamed up the most creative stories to prove their sincerity. The hospital patient flashed his I.D. bracelet to show me he was legit. I don't know how he got loose, but I hope they catch him before he gets too far away.

I was in Oakland for a book publishers' trade show. Even the participants had a flair for the grandiose. One fellow stopped by my display to discuss my need for a national publicist.

This man represents some of the biggest names in Hollywood, but my books drew him like a magnet. After dropping a few names like Joan Crawford and Gregory Peck, he launched into a series of questions about my public relations efforts.

"Television isn't my thing," I told him. "I'll leave the national tours to Newt and Mr. Powell."

"Okay, you may not be an Oprah guest," he said, "but there are hundreds of radio shows that would be perfect. You could do the interviews over the phone."

"Think of the orders you'd get on your '800' line!"

"I don't have an '800' line," I told him.

He seemed startled. "You don't have an '800' number?! Well, I hope you have a rich family," he quipped.

"I get by," I told him.

I should have said, "At least I don't have to live in Los Angeles," but I didn't think of it.

After the PR man wandered off, I turned to some folks standing next to me and said, "You know, if that guy represents people like Gregory Peck, how can he spend 20 minutes talking to me? You would think he'd have bigger fish to fry."

A week or two later, I received a letter from the PR man. He offered to "take sales of my terrific books to a new level." I assume he meant a higher level, but he didn't say.

His brochure mentions Glenn Ford, Chuck Norris, Michael Landon, Steve Allen, and Susan St. James as a few of the folks he has worked with over the years. Sports stars Bob Cousy, George Brett, Hakeem Olajuwan, and Tony Dorsett are in there, too.

Is this guy a name dropper, or what?

I hated myself afterward, but I wrote and told him I couldn't accept his offer right now. Maybe we could talk about it after deer season.

My letter was barely out the door when I regretted my hasty reply. Having my name in a brochure with ol' Greg and those other guys wouldn't be a bad thing.

At the very least I should have asked him to say "Hi" to Susan for me.

Tangled In The Net

It seems everyone is plugging the Internet these days. A person can't read two pages in a magazine or newspaper without running into the Internet.

I may be old fashioned, but I think I'll wait until promoters figure out what they're selling before I get too excited about the Internet and Information Super-Highway.

To me, the Internet is like a bad horse. You spend all day trying to catch the knothead; and then after you finally climb aboard, you can't for the life of you remember why you bothered.

Besides, what if a person gets on the Internet and can't get off? Readers might remember the old song about the guy who got on the Boston subway but didn't have change for his transfer?

He may ride forever 'neath the streets of Boston.
He's the man who never returned.
(Kingston Trio, I think.)

Of course the Internet accesses tons of information, but how good is the information? And what will we do with it after we get it? That's the big question.

Television provides mountains of information, too, but most of it isn't any good. Another load of nonsense on the Internet isn't going to help in that regard.

How do I know all of this? I saw it on television, that's how. Actually, I saw a heap of stupidity on television and have to wonder if the Internet might become just as bad.

The latest wrinkle in television is called "interactive news." Interactive news asks folks to call the TV station and vote on various issues.

I watched a segment recently in which callers were supposed to answer "Yes," "No," or "Don't care" to the question of the day.

The question was something like, "Should people more than 100 years old be required to wear helmets when riding their bicycles on the sidewalk?" (I know it's a dumb question, but it's all I could come up with.)

On this particular evening 75% of the callers answered, "Don't care."

What does that say about our society when 75% of the people who call to express an opinion say they don't have one? If they don't care, why are they calling?!

The newest variation on interactive news is for viewers to call "on-line" with their computer. The station's computer registers callers' opinions and broadcasts a few of them on the air.

The newscaster says, "Here's a response from Harvey Goshsakes down in Oldtown." Harvey says, "I don't know why we should furnish helmets for old people. If those people are going to ride bicycles, we'd better give helmets to the pedestrians."

One has to wonder, why is it better to talk with Harvey on the computer than to speak with him on the phone?

At least on the phone a person can say, "Hang it up, Harvey. And don't call back until you've had time to think about the question!"

Loosen Up

The increasing popularity of golf is creating new problems for golf addicts. A proliferation of new players has clogged fairways and slowed play to a turtle's trot on many courses.

A shortage of golf courses is part of the problem, of course, but slow play can be alleviated if folks will just remember two simple thoughts: Suspend the rules when necessary, and forget how the pros do it.

Of course everyone should play by the rules of golf when they can, but there has to be a limit. A person who hits a cow in the neighboring pasture with his tee shot, kills a woodpecker with his second, and then takes four swings in a sand trap, should be allowed to do anything he wants for the rest of the round.

New golfers and duffers like me can play just as fast as better golfers if we skip the practice swings, use cheap golf balls, and forget about the ones that go into the bushes. There comes a time when we just pick the ball up and say, "That's all the fun I need for this one, where's the next hole?"

I like to blame slow golfing on too much television. Watching and imitating the professionals has done more to slow down golf courses than anything I can imagine.

I can remember the days when a person would hit a golf ball, go find it, and hit it again. But now television has given each golfer a routine.

Today a person selects a tee from his bag, places the ball on the tee, and then walks around behind to see if it's straight. After lining up the shot in this manner, the golfer throws grass in the air to check the wind, grimaces into the sun like Gary Player, takes four practice swings, and then hits the ball.

All of this comes from imitating the pros on television. Standing behind the ball to line up the shot reminds one of Jack Nicklaus. Swinging the arms to loosen the shoulders imitates Fred Couples. I used to spit on my hands until I learned that started with Art Carney.

Weekend golfers think the pros do these things to relax and improve concentration. I think they do it just to irritate everybody else.

Golfers these days can be expected to line up the shot like Nicklaus, swing their arms like Couples, and hit the ball like Barney Fife. I don't know about others, but I can't even see a ball after Jack Nicklaus hits it; and every time my shoulders get loose I have to visit the chiropractor.

I'm not sure I can offer a solution to all of this, except possibly to suggest we keep the game in perspective; and try not to take it so seriously.

I agree with the comment of a famous golfer (whose name I can't remember). He said, "No one has fully mastered golf until he realizes his good shots are accidents, and his bad shots are good exercise."

Consumer Confidence

I see that consumer confidence is down again. That's one piece of news we can bank on. Consumer confidence is always down.

The last time consumers were confident they put everything on their credit cards. It may be some time before the exuberance returns.

That doesn't surprise me any. Consumer confidence is always low when the bills come due. Most folks lose their fiscal bravado several times a year.

I get a kick out of TV reporters interviewing Christmas shoppers in December. Each fall the reporters show up in shopping malls to get a grip on consumer sentiment.

They talk with storekeepers and shoppers to see how everyone feels about all the stuff they're buying. Then we hear about it on the evening news.

Invariably the news people show a lady with her arms full of packages saying, "Oh, I don't know. The economy is so bad, I don't think we are going to buy much this year."

I always want to shout, "Then, what are you doing in the

stores? Get out of the mall. Go home and save some money!"

That's kind of old fashioned, I guess. What is consumer confidence if not the ability to buy things we can't afford?

Just recently I read that consumer confidence is so puny these days that people are actually saving money. There's a vicious rumor for you. The last time folks saved their money was when Hector was a pup.

Those were the days before credit cards, government grants, and deficit financing. People paid cash, made do, and did without. It all seems sort of quaint now.

Several years ago my wife and I stopped at a little grocery in northern California to buy something for lunch. A sign behind the counter said, "Sorry, we cannot put deli sandwiches on credit." And a sign on the register said, "All grocery accounts must be paid by the 15th of each month."

"Can you imagine someone charging a sandwich?" I asked my wife. "If I couldn't afford a deli sandwich, I think I would find something a little less expensive to eat."

Then, we drove down the road to San Francisco and spent the night. The hotel charged us $15 to park the car overnight, and a cup of coffee cost 90 cents the next morning. Folks were running around like crazy, wanting $5 for this and $10 for that.

I kept thinking about the plight of the cities and their need for more funds, but I couldn't feel sorry for them. I can't imagine why city people choose to live the way they do.

I just wanted to ask, "Hey, what's the matter with you folks? If you'd move up the road a couple-hundred miles you could park your car for nothing — and pay cash for deli sandwiches with the money saved."

Wine Tasting

A news feature about French Syrah grapes reminded me of the futility of projecting one's tastes onto others. The news story quotes a winemaker as saying his French Syrah wine has the flavor of "black cherry and anise aromas, mingling with undertones of smoked bacon, spice and vanilla."

Now there's a man with some taste buds! I don't know much about wine, but that sounds like it would be good with scrambled eggs.

The winemaker's comments took me back to my wine tasting experience in the mid-70s. I was a county extension agent at the time, and each county with any kind of grape industry was asked to send an agent to the wine grape research update.

Imagine my chagrin when I learned the wine grape update was a couple of hours of research reports, followed by an afternoon of wine tasting.

This wasn't one of those wine and cheese events, either. This was a real "tasting" where each person is allotted a couple of glasses, water for rinsing his or her mouth, and a little can to spit in.

The object was to take a sip of wine, taste it, and spit it into the can. Then, you rinse your mouth with water before the next sample. It seemed a horrible waste to me, but who am I to criticize.

This group wasn't just a bunch of sheepherders, either. The gathering included winemakers, wine writers, and vineyard owners, plus a few dirt farmers and plain old county agents like Fred and me.

Fred sat across the room, but I could see he wasn't any more comfortable with this shindig than I was. He wasn't much of a wine drinker, either. Fred was a discreet sort of fellow who probably wouldn't eat a doughnut if he thought it might have salt in it.

I should stop here to explain, the wine grape industry was still young in our area, but the research station had been making wine for nearly 30 years. Most folks thought the researchers could make a good one if they would just stick with it a little longer.

So we were tasting the station's wines — and dutifully spitting them out, while the wine connoisseurs were waxing authoritative. "This one might be okay with cheese, but I'd like to see it with more ambiance and a bit more nose," one fellow said.

This went on for some time until we had tasted 30 wines or more. Then, a man from British Columbia's Okanogan Valley stood up and said, "I have a couple of cases in the trunk of my car, and I'd like for all of you to taste it."

He brought his wine into the room and explained it was made with a Riesling grape. He squeezed the grapes, put the juice and some yeast in a barrel, and left the whole thing in his basement a few months: No sulfites, no additives, just juice and yeast.

Eyebrows began to quiver as our Canadian friend poured his wine. The connoisseurs swirled it, and sniffed it, and held it up to the light. Someone commented the wine was a tad fruity and lacking in aroma.

That's when I looked over at Fred. I could see that Fred was still sipping, but he obviously stopped spitting a long time ago.

He took a sip of that Okanogan Valley wine and said, "Oh, what a bunch of baloney! As far as I'm concerned, this is the best darned wine we've had all day!"

Order Form

Pine Forest Publishing
314 Pine Forest Road
Goldendale, WA 98620
Phone: 509-773-4718

Quantity	Item	Price	Total
	It's Hard To Look Cool When Your Car's Full Of Sheep (Humor)	$11.95	
	Things that go "Baa!" in the Night (Humor)	$11.95	
	My Dog Was A Redneck, But We Got Him Fixed (Humor)	$11.05	
	Take the Kids Fishing, They're Better Than Worms (Humor)	$11.95	
	Livestock Showman's Handbook (Informational)	$17.95	
	Book Total		
	Postage & Handling: $2.00 per book		
	Washington residents: Please add 7% sales tax		
	Grand Total		

Payment must accompany order.
Please make checks payable to *Pine Forest Publishing*.

Name ____________________

Address ____________________

City ____________ State ________ Zip ________

Phone ____________________